Spiritual Self-Care
for Black Women

*The Complete Self-Help Guide Based
on Black Women's Spirituality*

2 Manuscripts in 1:
*Emotional Self-Care for Black Women,
Positive Affirmations for Black Women*

Dolores Maaike

TABLE OF CONTENTS

4

If this book will be to your liking,

please don't forget to leave

a short review on Amazon

_____

EMOTIONAL SELF-CARE FOR BLACK WOMEN

The Complete Guide With All the Techniques, Theories, and the Right Mindset to Master Your Emotions and Be Successful in Life

Dolores Maaike

Chapter 1: How Black Women Can Listen To Their Emotions And Welcome Them

How black women can Cultivate Self-Regulation To Manage Emotions

Self-regulation refers to your ability to control your impulses, emotions, and behavior carefully and tactfully so you don't act inappropriately.

When you as a black woman can successfully regulate your emotions and impulses, you don't let yourself easily or quickly become too jealous, angry, frustrated, stressed, depressed, or anxious. This helps you stay composed in high pressure and tensile situations and exhibit yourself as a strong and composed person. It also helps you stay strong even when things fail to go your way, or when you experience situations that lower your morale and self-esteem. This ensures you don't lose your self-confidence and esteem.

When you master the art of self-regulation, you keep your calm even when someone is lashing out at you and use your calmness to influence that person. This helps you win the hearts of people, cool down intense arguments, and successfully lead people.

An important component black women can recognize their own emotions is regulating them, called self-regulation in emotional intelligence. Self-regulation means that you halt or alter your emotions based on the perception that your emotions may lead to dysfunction for yourself or others. The reality is that emotions are a can of worms that can be positive and negative. We can feel love that leads us to behave beneficently towards others, or we may feel anger that causes us to do perhaps things that are not so beneficial.

Even love can cause you to do harmful or which should not be encouraged. Emotions are complicated. Changing things and being in touch with them does not necessarily mean that we are behaving in a way that leads to a positive result. The reality is that sometimes it is necessary to regulate our emotions. Indeed, assessing whether or not you may need to regulate your emotions is an important part of being in touch with your emotions, just as understanding the emotions of others is.

So how can you self-regulate? Let us find out:

Be Present With Your Emotion

When you experience a certain emotion, ensure you concentrate on it. If you feel envious of your friend who bought a new Mercedes, be present with that emotion and figure out how it makes you feel, why you feel that way, and how it influences your life. Don't respond to that emotion in the moment. Instead, closely observe as a third person viewing a certain situation.

Be Kind To Yourself

When you feel that a certain negative emotion brings you down, be kind and calm with yourself. Instead of criticizing yourself on why you feel terrible or why you feel the urge to lash out on someone, or why you negatively expressed your emotion, be gentle with yourself and tell yourself everything will be all right.

Focus On The Pros Of The Person

Get into the habit of noting and focusing on the positive traits and qualities of all the people you interact with regularly to remind yourself of those qualities whenever these people trigger certain unhealthy emotions in you. For instance, each time your spouse infuriates you, you can recall their positive traits, such as amicable and helpfulness. This will calm you before you blurt out something bad that will only aggravate the situation.

Practice Deep Breathing

Deep breathing soothes your stressed nerves, pacifies your raging emotions, and helps you vent your frustration through breath instead of words. Science shows that practicing *deep breathing* regularly helps you cultivate the habit of doing so all the time.

Naturally, when you breathe slowly and deeply, you use your breath to induce calmness. This allows you to manage your emotions successfully. For instance, if you feel stressed and angry, you can use your breath to turn these emotions into calmness. If you feel your anger might boil over, you can use your breath to become calm and use a peaceful way to express yourself.

Here's how you can use this strategy to practice self-regulation.

Sit in a quiet place. You can use your meditation spot for this purpose too.

Bring all your awareness to your breath just as you do while practicing mindfulness breathing meditation.

Now take deep breaths. Inhale through your nose to a count of five. This means you should count from 1 to 5 in your head as you inhale. Hold your breath in your lungs to a count of five and then exhale through your mouth to a count of five. If 5 is easy for you, inhale, exhale, and hold your breath to a count of 7 or even 10.

While you breathe deeply, make sure to inhale as much air as you can and exhale as much as possible. This makes you breathe fully and deeply.

Practice deep breathing using this strategy for about 2 minutes. Once you are through the practice, you'll feel much calmer and relaxed.

Practice this technique at least twice or even better, thrice a day. With time, breathe on a count of 7, 10, and 13 and so on, and increase the duration of your session from 2 minutes to 5, 7, and 10 and so on until you can do it for 15 or more minutes. This helps you develop the ability to breathe deeply at all times, which ensures you stay in control of your emotions all the time.

Slowly add these strategies into your life and be patient with yourself while waiting for the results. It takes time to master each technique and use it to yield results. Give yourself the gift of time and patience, and soon enough, you'll notice you are becoming better at managing your emotions.

How black women can Develop self-awareness

Every time as a black woman you should try as much as possible to keep in touch with every detail of your emotions, especially the negative ones. Doing this creates that self-awareness of yourself, thus increasing your personal touch within you. In most cases, even in various companies and other organizations, the most critical trait of a leader will always be self-awareness. That's the ability to monitor the emotions and reactions of everyone. Mastering self-awareness skills sometimes proves to be problematically sophisticated or difficult tasks. However, when you can find good ways to help you learn, this will help.

Remember, being an effective black woman needs much self-awareness than anything else. However, it is good to note that most of you will often avoid self-reflection, which can emulate you in knowing your self-awareness. You will end up getting feedback about your personality from various people. Nevertheless, in most cases, this will be full of honesty and flattery since no one would wish to tell you the real truth about yourself if, at all, it embraces some harmful elements. Along the process, you will not get a good perspective of your self-awareness from outside people. Therefore, because of these, you might harbor a low level of self-awareness without your knowledge.

Know Yourself and Observe Your Feelings

Feelings are part of black women's lives, and the best thing to do is acknowledge them. Taking a step in knowing yourself and realizing your feelings is the best step towards solving your emotions. That's the negative emotion that seems to engulf everyone, sending you into a world of pain and confusion. In most cases, black women have many failures when it realizes their negative emotions. Sadly, they will get overpowered by the negative emotions to the extent of failing to understand some burning issues of life.

In the end, they will get yourself living a fake life where you are even unable to know your identity. Getting to know your feelings will enable you to differentiate the negative emotions from the positive ones. Thus, you will be looking for appropriate ways to celebrate positive emotions as you eliminate the negative ones. By doing so, you will be taking control of your negative emotions and in the end, dealing with them, one by one. Remember, you need to know that living a lie will never take you far as this will soon come out in full glare. Therefore, in this topic, we will talk about how you can eventually know yourself. Below are illustrations that will help you understand yourself much better as a black woman.

You must know your personality

Getting to know your personality is a critical thing towards your self-awareness. Remember, you are already aware of the people around you. You also have a database about yourself. That's the one that talks much about your personality traits. You are also aware of those in your private life and the public cycle. The idea here is to understand your personality very well.

Get familiarized with your core values

Everyone has core values that enable them to get motivated every day. Core values refer to moral codes and those principles you hold in your heart. That's, there are more than eight core values that motivate us in many ways. In most cases, these values play a significant role in conflict resolution, persuading, influencing, decision making, communication, and even living your daily life.

Know your body

Knowing your body will help you comprehend much in your life. You will be able to control all those adverse reactions that might result from negative emotions. However, most people lack proper knowledge of their bodies. Therefore, the first step in dealing with negative emotions is making sure you understand the behavioral aspect of your body. Know when it reacts positively and when it does not.

Get to Know your Dreams

Your future depends on your hopes and those dreams that you emulate. They will always help you to establish that life you ever want. Knowing your goals well will enable you to control your negative emotions that might work against achieving or accomplishing them. And because of this, you will be working on all the instruments and other inputs that will help you make all these. Remember, everyone has a dream.

You should know your preferences

You should be in a position to understand your likes and dislikes. These are simple things that you can ignore in your life. Knowing what you like and struggling hard to maintain them will enable you to avoid even the negative emotions you might have in your life. Your dislikes, too, will allow you to workday in day out so that you can reduce them as little as possible. By doing this, you will be dealing with negative emotions such as frustrations, sadness, anxiety, and much more.

Use the Culture to Impact Emotions

Culture is different in all aspects of life, which will affect us when we set foot in another geographical ground with new cultures. Spotting tall buildings, the language of the natives, the air, and much more will have a more significant impact on our emotions. It is so funny that people tend not to understand that culture affects our feelings. According to them, emotions are those things that they manage to perform together with each other. That's, having negative emotions such as angriness implies that that emotion is living within you and the rest.

Recognizing and Managing Your Emotions

Black women need to be able to regulate the emotions and even change the way you feel so that you don't affect the people around you negatively. For instance, if you react negatively to something that someone has said crudely, you will attract unwanted attention and even risk your life while at it.

So, how do black women get to manage their emotions in the right way? Let us look at a few pointers to this fact:

Tune Into Your Feelings

This might seem simple but is very complicated. The most influential and critical skill of mastering your emotions is to be willing to tune into the emotion.

Many people fail to notice the moment until it is gone. Many times, we find ourselves disconnecting from our emotions in such a way that we don't make things work for us. To effectively manage your emotions, you need to notice when the emotions happen. Make sure you can pay attention to your feelings the right way before you can move ahead.

Rewind

When you tune into your emotions, you need to take a few steps backward. Ask yourself how you got to the situation that might have contributed to those feelings and then go after them,

Once you understand where the emotions are coming from, you will manage them the right way. When you take notice of your emotions, you will be able to look for the various triggers that may have taken you into the feelings in the first place.

Gain the Right Perspective

Once you understand your feelings, the next thing is to step out of the zone and then gain a better perspective. Consider what might happen if you continue in the same vein. What will happen if you stay on the same route you are following?

Will, the consequences of your actions, affect you solely, or will they affect other people as well? You need to take time and consider whatever matters most to you at that moment. When you gain the right perspective and understand the feelings when you return to your present moment will make it easier for you to move ahead.

Become Self Aware

You cannot manage your emotions when you aren't aware of yourself. You need to tune in and gain a broader perspective of your emotions. You need to take things deeper and zoom into the moment. Although everyone experiences emotions, the unique experience is subjective in all ways. When you become self-aware, you will understand yourself and come up with the best coping skills.

Listen to the Voices in Your Head

What do you hear? Do you hear anything in your head or your mind? If you can listen to whatever it is, then enumerate it. Give it a name and a volume. Listening to the different voices within your inner self will help you assess the connections between thoughts and feelings. When we are in social situations, especially conflicts, we often make our narrative louder than others.

Change What You Can

You need to cut down on the triggers of the emotion, and you will find that you experience emotions less frequently. This can include cutting down on stress at work, changing negative thought patterns that you experience, and practicing better communication.

Finding an Outlet

When you make changes in your life, you can cut down on any negative emotions that you experience. When you find an outlet, you also eliminate any stress triggers that you might have. When you make changes in your life to reduce the frustration, you will find healthy outlets that will deal with the emotions.

There are various outlets that you can use to release the negativity. These include:

- Regular exercise gives you an emotional lift and the right outlet for your negativity.
- Meditation will help you find much-needed inner peace that you can work with. This will make your emotions less overwhelming.
- Find various opportunities to have a lot of fun and get more laughter into your life so that you relieve stress and change the perspective of your emotions.
- You don't have to stick to these outlets; you can create your own to find something that works best for you.

Experience the Emotions, but Don't Get Stuck in Them

Managing emotions doesn't mean that you suppress them. What you need to do in such a case is to try and experience the emotion and then let it go. Don't put your mind or feelings to it because it will destroy you.

How black women can Change Emotions

Emotions form an essential part of human beings, and everyone must understand how to handle them. Most individuals do not like them, especially the negative emotions that may cause anger, pain, sadness, and the like. Because everyone tries to avoid unpleasant feelings, it is common for people to suppress negative feelings, yet this is not advisable. They see such emotions as problems that need to be resolved. However, emotions occur naturally, and it is impossible to suppress them.

The ultimate solution to managing unpleasant feelings lies in learning how to manage one's emotions. Doing this enables you to handle and manage your moods and feelings successfully. The process involves accepting a person's emotional state and managing each emotion as it arises.

There are several ways black women can control your mood, feelings, and emotions. Let us check out some of them:

Label Each Emotion

If you would like to manage your emotions effectively, you must first start by acknowledging their existence and any effects they are causing on you. For instance, you need to establish whether you feel disappointed, nervous, excited, or afraid. Note that some emotions may occur as a result of another hidden passion. For instance, a feeling of anger may be due to an action that left you vulnerable or wasted. Dig deep to understand what is exactly happening inside you. Give a label to every emotion that you experience. This is because some people experience multiple emotions simultaneously.

Adjust Your Way of Thinking

Most emotions always affect a person's thought pattern. For instance, if you are anxious about something and the person causing the anxiety calls, you may start thinking that something negative will occur. If you are enthusiastic about someone and the person contacts you, you will only develop positive thoughts about what the person will say to you.

Engage in Suitable Activities

Each time a black woman is faced with a challenge that is causing you to have a foul mood, do not continue to engage in things that make the situation worse. Instead, get some activities that can help uplift your spirit and participate in them. Do something that makes you happy like listening to music, taking a walk, meditating, and visiting a friend. Most individuals use vigorous activities such as martial arts and boxing, to control their emotions.

Avoid Instant Reaction

When it comes to negative emotions, you shouldn't react immediately. This is because when you are angry or in fear, you will always do or say regrettable things. To achieve this, always take a deep breath and relax when faced with a tough situation. Continue doing this for as long as you feel overwhelmed by the emotion, or until you feel that your heart rate has gone back to normal.

Seek Guidance

Most black women find the solution to their feelings by expressing themselves to others. You can release your negative emotions to others healthily and acceptably by doing this. Share your feelings with people you trust so that they can advise you accordingly. Recount the occurrences that triggered the emotion and hear what others say. This will launch a new perspective on the whole issue, and you can use this insight to manage your thoughts and reactions.

Broaden Your Perspective

Every situation always has a bigger picture that you can focus on. Understand that everything happens with a reason. This will help you see the purpose of any situation instead of focusing on the negative aspects involved. For some circumstances, you may not understand the meaning at the time of occurrence, but as days go by, you may start seeing the reason why things happened as they did.

Practice Forgiveness

The people around you can trigger some emotions. Some may be close relations like family members or friends. You can even cause negative emotions by yourself. It is essential that when this happens, you get to forgive the person that triggered the emotion. When you hold a grudge against others, the negative emotion will keep surfacing each time you see the person. Forgiveness detaches you from the negative emotion and gives you peace even when others wrong you.

Always Anticipate a Negative Emotion

It will be a lie for you to believe that life will always be pleasant all through for black women. And that you can live a life that is free of pain. Some people seem to be happy all the time. However, this does not mean they do not experience any negative feelings, and it only means that such people have learned to manage their emotions more effectively. Therefore, always expect some negative feelings to arise as you go about your day-to-day activities.

Be Flexible

It is almost impossible to control how and when emotions occur when it comes to emotions. You need to remain open to these as they occur. Allow them to occur at any time and anywhere. Only seek ways to balance them to not mess in your actions.

View any negative feelings as an opportunity to improve on yourself. These may be feelings such as fear, anger, jealousy, and anger. Focus on the positive aspect of such feelings, take them as your areas that need development.

Do Not Neglect Any Feelings

Learn how to tolerate any unpleasant sensations. Do not avoid or ignore them. Instead, keep reflecting on the experience and any changes occurring in your body due to such feelings. Keep reminding yourself that millions of people around the globe face the same kind of feelings. As you do this, ensure that you do not play any blame games towards others. Blaming other people for your negative emotions can hinder them from genuinely interacting with you.

Generally, managing emotions is not an easy affair. Sometimes, some feelings may get out of control however much you try. However, the more you practice how to regulate your emotions, the more stable you become when it comes to handling them. With time, you will build your confidence around people and adverse circumstances, since it will be easy for you to overcome most of the challenges that you encounter.

Ways of Dominating Your Emotions
Practice staying calm

Maintaining composure is necessary for black women to manage stressful situations. In practice, how we process negative emotions can differentiate between being reactive and assertive. It is advisable to exercise when under duress to maintain calmness.

Exhibit assertiveness

One of the sources of negative emotions is the reluctance to define and enforce boundaries. It is often necessary to specify boundaries in life to state your stand. For instance, one of the situations that demand taking a stand is exercising the right to disagree, stating your priorities, and protecting yourself from danger and duress.

Remain proactive when handling a difficult person

At some point, you handled a difficult individual that you deemed unreasonable. You might have faced a colleague that you labeled difficult at the workplace. Most people loathe the experience with a person they consider as difficult. Fortunately, there are multiple ways to remain proactive in difficult contexts. Start by taking a deep breath when you feel irritated and upset with an individual before you act or say something and count slowly to ten. In most scenarios, before you reach ten, you will have figured out a better way to express the issue than you would have done before handling the emotion. The intent of all this is to review the issue when calm.

Mastering Your Emotions

Mastering your emotions is the key skill black women must attain to become emotionally intelligent. It is the most crucial to further development and improvement.

Here are a few ways black women can master their emotions:

1) First identify what you are feeling. Do you feel angry or is something else bothering you? You need to get clarity on the emotion and question it. We often feel angry, but we don't know the cause. We assume we know the cause, but we have no idea in the end. Most likely we are transferring our anger from something onto something else.

2) Second acknowledge and appreciate your emotions. Be grateful for your emotions. Know that your emotions support you through your life. Be thankful that they are guiding you and giving you a secret message. This message only you can see. Be happy that you can feel and are emphatic. Some people are closed off and have no inner connection with their emotions. But you, you do! So use your inner connection and understand the message.

3) Get curious about the message this emotion is giving you. Ask these questions. What else could this mean? What can I learn from this? How do I want to feel? What am I willing to do about it? Ask yourself these, and wait for an answer. How do you want

to solve this problem? How can I learn from this? Have I felt this before? If so, what did I do back then to solve it?

4) Get confident. This hint has been mentioned several times throughout the book. This is the fastest, simplest and most powerful way to handle any emotion! You need to be confident. Your emotions will strengthen over time once you have the confidence to improve them. You will develop an entirely new way of thinking.

5) Accept that you can handle this not only today but also in the future. Remember how you handled this type of situation before and repeat the action. Try to change your perception and know that you can do it. Know that you are not giving up or backing down. Know that you are a warrior. Know you can do anything you put your mind to.

6) Get excited and take action. Take some action and control your emotions. Remember it is important to take care of the emotion when it first starts, not when it has tripled in size. If you leave the emotion unattended, you will soon be fighting a huge monster, instead of a little one.

Challenge the Negative Thoughts and Replace them with Positive Ones

It is only when you become aware of your negative thoughts, challenge them, and constantly replace them with positive substitutes that you train yourself to control your extreme emotions and move past them. Here is how black women can do this:

Every time you find yourself catastrophizing the severity of an instance, reading too much into things, reducing someone who hurt you to a two dimensional label, and making negative predictions about things you do not feel too excited about, question the authenticity of those thoughts and emotions.

Also, every time you think negatively about yourself or nurture a deep, negative belief about your capabilities, think of the emotion that stirred up those thoughts and beliefs and question their authenticity. If you feel you cannot win a competition, why do you think that is? If you believe that it is because you do not work hard, you know exactly what you must do to prove yourself wrong: work hard. It is important to find out the root cause of a negative thought and then address it to manage the negative thoughts and the underlying emotions causing them.

Once you are done analyzing a negative thought or belief, find a more realistic and positive substitute of it and repeat it over and over again. For example, if you thought, 'I don't think I'll ever reach the break-even point in my business and forever struggle with improving the sales', change it to something along the lines of, 'My goal maybe difficult, but it is possible - especially if I work hard to achieve it.' Such realistically positive thoughts make you nurture hope and feel positive. When something is affirmed to your subconscious, it accepts it and slowly shapes thoughts in that direction. Hence, if you frequently feed positive suggestions to your subconscious and think about them day in and day out, you will soon get rid of all the unhealthy thoughts and emotions and replace them with healthy and positive ones.

Chapter 2: How Black Women Can Develop Emotional Intelligence

What Is Emotional Intelligence?

Emotional intelligence determines how good you can understand other people and their emotions and how you can find a way to work with them to maximize cooperation. If you can't manage your and other people's emotions and appropriately react to them, the chances are that success will go by you. Emotional intelligence is what can make you easily 'fit into the group' and keep a bunch of interpersonal relationships at a high level.

Aside from that, it also enables you to understand yourself better, which means that you will be able to adapt to stressful situations better and avoid depression and other negative emotions. It is equally important to assess what you feel and what others feel.

Improved psychological satisfaction: Individuals who use emotional intelligence show more self-esteem, are more satisfied with life, and are often free of the anxiety and depression that plagues others.

Improved academic performance: Studies suggest that highly emotionally intelligent people perform better in academics as rated by their teachers.

Improved social interactions in business settings: Some research has suggested that highly emotionally intelligent people are better at negotiating deals and in social dynamics in general in the workplace.

Better perception by peers: People who cultivate emotional intelligence are perceived more positively than those with less emotional intelligence. This has been shown to include perceptions of social skills and friendliness.

Improved personal and romantic relationships: High emotional intelligence is correlated with more successful intimate relationships and relationships with family members.

Generally improved social interactions: Much of emotional intelligence measurement and assessment comes from reports by individual. These assessments find that high emotional intelligence correlates with better social skills, better relationships with others, more pacific relationships, and less conflict.

Physical well-being: Managing stress and taking care of our bodies is key to our general well-being. Emotional intelligence is tied to our ability to take care of our bodies and managing stress and this can have an impact on our overall wellness. Being aware of your reaction to stress and your emotions will help you maintain good health and minimize stress in your daily life.

Relationships: Communicating your feelings constructively can be achieved when you better understand and manage your emotions. It also makes it easier to communicate with people you relate with. Understanding what the people you care about need or feel or how they respond fosters a stronger and better relationship.

Mental health: Emotional intelligence greatly affects our attitude and perspectives about life. Having a high level of emotional intelligence is linked to a happy life because it helps to reduce anxiety, depression and mood swings.

Success: Having high emotional intelligence helps you be stronger at motivating yourself, resulting in reduced procrastination and improved self-confidence. It will also help you form a stronger connection with people around you, build a strong network of support, overcome obstacles and persist in the face of tough situations. Success becomes easier to attain when you can delay gratification and visualize the result you want.

Resolving conflicts: It is much easier to resolve issues with other people or even avoid them before they start when you can recognize their emotions and identify with their standpoint. It also allows you to negotiate the situation better because you can understand what other people want. Giving people what they want is easier when you know what it is.

Leadership: A successful leader can perceive what his followers need to meet those needs in a way that increases productivity and work-environment fulfillment. The capacity to comprehend what influences others, relate positively, and establish a better rapport with others in the work environment makes those with higher emotional intelligence better leaders. An honest leader is always ready to bring people together and build a team by deliberately using each person's emotional intelligence to profit the group.

Emotional intelligence is not a skill we use only around our friends or family. It is used in our daily life. From the moment we wake up to the moment we close our eyes to sleep, we constantly need to employ our emotional intelligence. It is important for different sectors of our lives.

How black women Can Become Emotionally Intelligent

Observe

The first step towards increasing your Emotional Intelligence is observation. You are the first-hand witness of your emotions and must stay completely aware while experiencing the different types of emotion in your life. While every action has an equal and opposite reaction in physics, this law rarely holds in human psychology. Our reactions vary with time, place and situation. There is no set rule in which man reacts or feels in any given circumstance. This variation in reaction occurs primarily because of the intangible nature of our emotions.

Listen to your body

The human body is linked with the mind and often the mind responds to the body as well. When the body experiences a fall, it is no wonder that the mind stops thinking about everything else, concentrating entirely on breaking the fall. Similarly, when the mind is worked up and tensed when involved in a heated argument, we experience adrenaline in our gut and our heart rate increases sharply. Thus the body is responding continuously to our emotions. Every Black woman should learn to read his body properly to understand the mind. The body keeps sending signals and indications about the mental makeover of the person. Observe closely how your body reacts to the sharp changes in your moods, feelings and emotions and learn to identify your emotions through the signs shown by the body.

Read your behavioral pattern

Behavior is how we conduct ourselves and act or react towards our environment. Psychology has long ago established a connection between our emotions and our behavior. There is no direct or indirect relationship since the emotions are not one way but we experience millions of emotions in just a day most of which we cannot even account for. These emotions when collected together define a person's general behavior in life. We avoid chatting to people we feel are irritable because we can foresee ourselves snapping at them.

Emotions are natural

Behavior can be seen as another form, of action and they stem directly more often than not from our emotions. If we label our emotions, it becomes impossible to understand the pros and cons of our emotions and the behavior it induces in our lives. If one cares enough to look deeper and discover the source of these emotions and actions, then one can gain a deeper insight into the world of emotions, making them emotionally intelligent.

Develop Emotional Intelligence

You may not have learned this kind of intelligence in school, but emotional intelligence is just as important (if not more) as academic smarts.

This is the only *real* way black women can fine-tune their emotions, to learn the subtle differences between each experience so they become somewhat of a sommelier when it comes to emotions.

Once your brain can comprehend, anticipate and categorize the sensations that you feel more accurately, you'll be able to tailor your responses and actions to suit the situation.

Built Resilience

Having a better mindset will involve you working on building up your resilience. This means that you will have to become a more determined individual, to no longer let challenges and setbacks affect you mentally and emotionally. To keep persisting even when things are difficult. Building up your resilience until you are a stronger person mentally and emotionally will help you control your anger in a way that you were never able to before.

Keep Checking In

No matter what situation you find yourself in, always remember to stop and check in with yourself.

- How am I feeling?
- Am I still able to control my emotions?
- How do I feel right now around this person or situation?

Close your eyes and take a couple of measured deep breaths, remind yourself to focus on your present, and shift your mind away from what is threatening to trigger your emotions.

Even when you've eventually learned how to get a good handle on your emotions, it's still good to check in with yourself now and then.

Don't Shift the Blame

If you're always looking for an opportunity to blame someone else, to eagerly shift the blame so you don't have to feel as bad about losing control, you need to keep working on your emotional intelligence. That person may have provoked your emotions, but the way you chose to react was still *your decision*. No one forced you into it, that was completely your decision and yours alone. You need to accept partial responsibility for what happened, even if that person was at fault if they intentionally provoked you (some people don't realize what they're doing).

Change Your Focus

Whenever faced with a situation that aggravates your emotions, try switching your focus. Direct your attention to something else, preferably something that will make you feel better and immediately take your mind off what was bothering you earlier. The more focused the unpleasant emotion, the worse it seems to become by the minute. We can't help it, somehow we get sucked into the vortex of emotions, especially when they are negative, and they just seem to have a much stronger pull over us.

Find an Outlet

Emotions need to be released in one way or another. Once you've managed to control it, you need to release it (not suppress it). Every black woman should find an activity that allows them to release your emotions healthily.

Exercise is one way of channeling your emotions in a way where no one gets hurt. The bonus there is you feel better and get fitter while you're at it. Meditation and yoga are two forms of relaxation that help you return the calm and tranquility to your mind.

Immerse yourself in a hobby or a passion that soothes and release you.

Keeping a journal for example, means releasing your emotions instead of lashing out at others.

Painting your emotions is another approach to take, and it can be any activity that makes you feel better and acts as a release form.

As long as you can say *I feel so much better!* After you've done it, that's good enough for a start.

Make It Your Commitment to Change

Having a valid reason will help you stay on course as you work towards improving your emotions.

- Why is it important for you to make this change?
- Why did you decide to commit to this process?

These are questions you must answer with clarity, conviction, and remind yourself of the reason to keep going when you start to encounter obstacles along the way.

Knowing your *"Why"* is how you remind yourself to keep moving forward, and there will be many moments during this journey when you're going to need it.

Controlling your emotions requires a deep commitment from you, and that commitment is going to come from your reason *why.*

How black women can improve their emotional intelligence

Managing emotions helps to be more open to new, different feelings. This is how, ultimately, you want to work with emotions. But to be able to do that, you need to focus on improving your EQ.

Self-awareness

Self-awareness can be cut short to three main categories: emotional awareness, accurate self-assessment and self-confidence.

First, you can self-evaluate the emotions you feel the most and how you usually react to them, so you can begin to identify your emotional strengths and weaknesses. Then, try to label your emotions. Recognize, understand and name them. It will make I easier for you to pause when needed, and take the time to think about how to react. If you know what you are dealing with, you can respond accordingly after reflection.

Self-management

For self-regulation, understand first that everyone has a choice regarding how we react to situations. Maybe you want to categorize emotions as good and bad, but there are no such things as good and bad emotions. How you react to these emotions however is what matters the most.

Use everything around you to try to monitor your feelings. Are you sweating more than you were five minutes ago? Has your heart rate increased rapidly? Do you feel blood rushing to your cheeks? Try to balance your emotions by letting the uncomfortable moment go away. Feelings and emotions come and go, but you know that your deep, balanced state is calmness. Let the temporary feeling go away and find your balance back.

Your goal should never change. If you need to adapt something, it's the way you see and think about it. If you don't think it's possible, don't quit, search a mentor and ask for advice on what your next move should be. But always remember to manage your goal yourself. Simply put, stick to the goal, but adapt. And always celebrate small victories, you don't climb the Everest with taking only one step, but you need to take that one step to do it many times.

Empathy

You can only become more empathetic as a black woman by hanging out with people. But if you want to improve your levels of empathy, you need to start to hang out with strangers. You probably already know how your friends react to your presence, so meeting new people and spending time with them can only be beneficial. You will be able to hear about different experiences and put your own life experience into a new perspective.

Be open to good and bad experiences, for yourself and others. That way, you will be able to put yourself in someone else's shoes easier. Listen to people when they talk to you, and observe them. Pay attention to their words of course, but also their gestures and their body language. Also, show sensitivity and see how they react to your actions to learn to adapt.

Social skills

Verbal and non-verbal communications are key here. Black women need to learn to choose your words wisely. You can't have only one way to deal with customers or people. Your words and moves need to be tailored to the person you interact with. You can't act the same when you want to sale a car and when you listen to someone talking about their children. Practice techniques of salespeople if you work in that branch and learn what to say about children. It seems like a mammoth task to learn all these different ways of acting, but it's worth it.

Improving your emotional intelligence may look like intimidating at first, but it's worth the hard work and the discomfort you're going to put yourself into. You will have an edge on most people out there since most of them somehow still want to ignore the power of emotional intelligence.

Chapter 3: Why managing emotions is crucial for black womens' success at work and in business.

Environmental Impact on black womens' Emotions

Nearly every sane person wants to be in an environment where one feels respected, appreciated, and listened to and this involves people. When a colleague or manager does not appear to understand your unique situation, chances are that you are likely to feel not valued and may feel ignored. When people around you exhibit high levels of emotional intelligence, you are likely to express positive emotions. If the people around you appear not to be listening and understanding, chances are that you are likely to feel disrespected and ignored.

Additionally, some people might purposely provoke black women to exhibit negative emotions. Think of a supervisor that insists on shorter deadlines while ignoring your reason that the deadline is inhumane and impractical. Think of a colleague who makes fun of your ethnicity or religion when you clearly indicated that you are discouraged. All these actions are done to provoke you further, leading to your being more emotional than you should. It is important to be around mature, open-minded, and understanding people's actions can aggravate negative feelings. In most cases, our anger and other negative feelings are normally directed at people or what people did.

Did you know that your surroundings can affect the way you feel and your emotions? The surrounding isn't all about the people around you, but rather the ambiance that surrounds your life. If you are surrounded by positivity, then you will be happier, if instead you are surrounded by negativity, you will find it hard to live your life.

Therefore, it is upon you to create that perfect environment in your home or at the office so that you can be happier, thrive, be more focused, and relax.

It is a clear fact that the environment you set will affect your productivity, mood, as well as your creativity.

Your surrounding affects your performance and mood. When you learn how the surroundings affect you, you can work things to your advantage. So, the key to learning about the various skills to create the best environment lies in understanding the starting point.

Changing Emotion with Environment

Black womens' environment has a huge impact on their mood, particularly if you are empathetic. You draw on the mood around you and feed off of it—if the mood is tense and apprehensive, you are also bound to absorb that apprehension. You will be afraid of the environment if you feel dangerous, and you will be sad in an environment filled with others that are sad.

This is why it is so incredibly important to be mindful of the kinds of company you keep. They need to keep good company that is kind to you and respectful if you want to keep a happy mood. If you want to be calm and relaxed, feeling confident in your surroundings, you need to be in an environment conducive to exactly that—calm and relaxation. Your body will be clued in on how to behave based on how others behave. You will calm down when the body language of others says that there is nothing to be afraid of. You will feel energized if those around you appear to be energized as well.

If you want to change your emotions, you should stop to look at your environment. Is it strict? Is it harsh and uncomforting? Do you feel loved or safe? If you cannot answer that you are happy and comfortable in your relationship, it is time to consider removing yourself from the toxic environment.

Toxic environments only breed more toxicity. Negative environments only breed negativity. It is okay to cut that negativity and toxicity out of your life, no matter how familiar or comfortable it is. Your mental health will thank you for it if you do so.

Further, if you want to influence your mood to be happier and energized, you should surround yourself with good energy. Surround yourself with good friends. Put on some energetic music that gets you in the mood to move. You are far more likely to enjoy yourself if the environment around you is conducive to enjoying it.

Ultimately, you will have to recognize that your emotions are linked to your environment. Your emotions will almost always reflect whatever environment you have surrounded yourself with, which is okay. However, if you are in a toxic environment, you owe it to yourself and your loved ones to fix that. You do not have to put up with toxic individuals, even if they are family. You are well within your rights to end a relationship from someone, familial, romantic, or platonic if you feel it is a toxic environment that needs to be left.

While on the topic of environments, if black women are being abused in any way or feel unsafe at home, there are resources for you that can help you escape. Please look up your local domestic violence hotline if you feel safe and ask for help. No matter how difficult it may feel for you, you can get out alive and flourish somewhere you are meant to grow instead of being stunted and barely surviving somewhere toxic. People change their emotions when they make some simple changes to their environment.

How Black women can Learn to Cope with Criticism

Criticism in life is never fun, whether this criticism is emerging from your friends, teachers, or even your parents. More so, some blame can be constructive, which will only help you improve your personality. However, if it brings you down or works against your principals, you need to shed it off like a plague. Criticism itself brings about negative emotions such as frustrations, sadness, anger, and sometimes you might feel low self-esteem. Lack of confidence and less value of yourself will crop in your life, killing every positive mood within you. However, if well controlled and managed, you will be able to deal with the negative emotions that come with it.

Black women should first know the real difference between constructive and destructive. Understanding the difference is the initial step in dealing with the nagging criticism. You must be able to evaluate all your feedback, and again, you must know whoever is giving out the input. If it comes from your superiors like teachers, tutors, professors, and so on, then it might mean positive. That's, they are only looking for a better part of you and want you to improve. However, when this comes from haters, people who are frenemies, and even enemies, you must consider it in several ways.

In most cases, our enemies or haters will only see the negative side of our goals and actions. They have the audacity of saying bad things about yourself, and you get frustrated and dull at the end of the day. Some frenemies derive pleasure at your downfalls. They are people locked in your friend zone and will laugh with you during the day and derive pleasure at night, especially when you are failing. Therefore, knowing the difference will enable you to choose what to follow. Remember, constructive criticism has the power to help you, while destructive one will only cause more damage and hurt. Following your choice will enable you to have control of your criticism, thus helping you deal with your negative emotions.

You have to accept that you are not perfect. The best way to deal with criticism involves your understanding about your imperfections. No one is perfect in this world, and how we handle our defects will help us delete the motions of perfectionism, which hurts our emotions. In this case, you have to expect any form of feedback since no one is always perfect. People have serious issues relating to flaws and defaults. Hence, if you cannot identify your weaknesses, you are making a mistake in your analysis of yourself. Therefore, in this case, you can list your flaws and look at the ones you have to improve. Remember, you should not feel wrong about this exercise since this is to help you realize that there is still room for improvement.

Never take anything personally. Taking everything personally will never help to deal with any form of criticism. That's, it will only escalate it into greater heights. Sometimes at the workplace, your boss might comment on something about you. At some point, you will think it is not right, but remember, according to him, he only wants the best from you. By saying such, he will only require you to step up your game and improve. Again, your friend might accuse you of zoning out when you are in a conversation. The friend is not calling you a horrible and careless person but only wants you to respect the conversation. Remember, if the criticism is positive, then you will realize many results when you follow it; however, at some points, some might be destructive, which will only pull you down completely. In this case, you must shed them off entirely. Dealing with criticism will enable you to take control of your negative emotions.

You should stop being much sensitive. Some people tend to cry, have sorts of upsets, and even feel very low and defensive, especially when they get feedback. Thus, they aren't aware that feedback is part of our lives, and we need to look for ways to accept every type of feedback, whether it is positive or negative. I know most frenemies, haters, and those who want the worst for us will give back destructive feedback. You need to be less sensitive in situations like this. The best way is to focus on this feedback and identify several ways that you can use to avoid any pain brought by it. You can also work on your reputations since they matter much to you and the people in your surroundings. Look at several ways to offer control over your emotions and don't get swayed away by the wind of negative feedback from the people. By doing this, you will be controlling your negative feelings to better your present and future life.

How black women can Overcome Negative Emotions at the Workplace

Most research on this subject focuses on how families of origin create legacies of self-criticism and low self-esteem in black women. Still, it's not just our immediate families that influence how we perceive ourselves. Their self-esteem in childhood and adulthood is also impacted by things they experience in external settings. These experiences can occur within their relationships and what they witness in the world around them. Interactions with teachers, coaches, peers, friends, extended family, and even strangers all can impact their self-esteem.

Emotions have always been in the workplace even though they have been kept within proper limits, with some people pretending not to feel anything whenever they are at work.

Not surprisingly, things like bullying, abuse, and dealings with narcissistic people create vulnerabilities about self-esteem. Additionally, overt or even implied criticism or ridicule by anyone we encounter can make us question our value.

Did you experience any of these things in childhood? Check the boxes if applicable:

- Abuse (physical, emotional, sexual)
- Criticism
- Ridicule
- Bullying
- Dealing with a narcissist
- Dealing with somebody irrational

To complicate matters, the same things that challenge our self-esteem can also *become* challenges in and of themselves when self-esteem is not in a healthy place. Things like dating, working, taking on responsibilities, and interacting with different people open us to new experiences that can shape our self-esteem. If self-esteem is already low, navigating these experiences can be difficult. Without a foundation of healthy self-esteem, even simple interactions can perpetuate doubt about who we are as we continue to interpret and assign negative meaning to every interaction and internalize this negativity.

Envy

One of the common workplace emotions is envy and the emotion is allowed to manifest as each one of us admires to be accomplished. It is allowed for human beings to nurse and pursue ambitions routinely. However, when one becomes uneasy with the achievement of others to the point of being affected mentally and physically, the feeling is envy. Like any other mental condition, envious persons rarely accept that they have a negative emotion. Envy is likely to affect the workplace negatively. Even though a limited and occasional form of envy is welcome as a necessary trigger to improve and strive, it becomes an adverse emotion if it becomes unmanaged. Since workplaces appraise their employees, individual employees are likely to admire accomplishing more like their feted colleagues, which can breed feelings of envy.

Nervousness

Another common feeling at the workplace regarded as negative is feeling nervous or worried. For emphasis, feeling nervous is welcomed as part of human feelings. Still, like any emotion regarded as negative, it should be handled to avoid creating an adverse impact on work relations and output. One of the ways you will notice when feeling nervous is that you become restless. If feeling worried, your mind is stuck on what could go wrong, which elicits fear, especially the worst-case scenarios that replay on your mind. Expectedly, you will try to elicit multiple courses of action within a short period, making you more unease to the point that your uneasiness manifests in actions.

Anger

Anger might be one of the commonest negative emotions at the workplace and this is expected. Workplaces have targets and evaluate their workers, which creates pressure and deadlines. When workers are under pressure and defined expectations judge the value, they are likely to act under pressure. When one is pushed to the limit by deadlines, an individual may react impulsively by clicking, walking away, or banging the table. Workers are also evaluated on the contribution to overall productivity. When workers feel the scoring system is unfair, they are likely to feel agitated. Anger can then be acknowledged as a negative emotion when one cannot satisfy the expectations at an individual and public level.

Dislike

Dislike is one of the negative emotions that is overlooked and sometimes misinterpreted as something else. In this context, dislike refers to the general and unjustified feeling of disassociating and disinterest in someone or something. At one point, you might have disliked someone or some movie character without any reason for feeling that. Dislike needs no justification just like love. Some dislikes are driven by social bias that eventually reinforces your personal bias. For instance, you might have just disliked the new worker even before you met or interacted. When you try to look for the reasons for disliking the innocent, you do not get any. Dislike is a risk to developing social relationships, as it denies you objectively assessing other individuals, which will affect your productivity and theirs.

Disappointment

Disappointment, like anger, is a common negative feeling at the workplace. Feeling disappointed is unavoidable at the workplace due to needing to accomplish targets or fit in a certain circle. When a good-intentioned worker fails to reach the set target or attain an average score during the appraisal, the person is likely to feel unhappy. The feeling is initially welcome as it can motivate the person to self-evaluate and commit to delivering more in the next cycle. Unfortunately, the feeling of being disappointed can persist and cause adverse effects to the individual's self-esteem, including negatively affecting the person's social life. When you continuously feel disappointment, you are also likely to express anger which might negatively affect your relationships.

Trauma

Trauma arises when one goes through a disturbing event and feels overwhelmed. For instance, near-death injury and torture can trigger trauma. Trauma should be acknowledged and viewed as an acute stress event. Like any mental health issue, the first step to manage it is to accept that it is present. Several affected people might not accept that they are suffering from trauma or not understand that they have trauma. The initial step to coping with trauma is to help individuals acknowledge that they are suffering from trauma. It is important to underscore that trauma is a way of the mind forcing you to seek closure from a disturbing experience to restore balance.

How Good Emotions Can Guide black women to Financial, Loving and Personal Success
Career

Many black women experience negative interactions with others before beginning a career. Post-secondary education is a time of great growth for many women, with the possibility of increased confidence and autonomy. This can also be a time of further exposure to societal norms and romantic relationships, reinforcing or decreasing self-confidence. Learning experiences during this time are not limited to the classroom.

These experiences continue with the development of a career. Job searching, interviewing, and adjusting to new expectations while managing a family or social life can tremendous pressure on women. We are bombarded by the idea of "having it all" (i.e., being superwoman), which can be encouraging (because, yes, women can do anything) but can also lead to feelings of failure when we are held to impossible standards and unrealistic expectations.

The workplace can be a landmine of confidence busters, including being excluded from a social event, being passed up for a promotion, or making an error. Don't even get me started on the many other offenses black women can face, such as pay disparity, pumping breast milk in a closet (or, worse, a restroom), sexual harassment, impossible expectations of the work–life balance, and so on.

Emotions and Finances

On the positive side, certain emotions can make it easier for black women to take risks. Black women who can process negative emotions and show moderate positive emotions may take risks and invest in the stock market. To take risks, they must be mentally prepared for both positive and negative success. In other terms, one must exhibit the ability to handle negative emotions and recover in good time. People with a positive outlook are likely to take risks even when the market is not performing to expectations. If you feel energized, confident, and hopeful, then taking a risk and investing is not a big deal. Marketers understand this and will invest time in eliciting the right emotions before inviting you to buy their stock.

Relationships

If you as a black woman surround yourself with negative people, you will become increasingly negative. If you associate with women who backstab, gossip, and compare, your self-confidence will be adversely affected. It is difficult to be around someone who is always complaining because she may not welcome or appreciate any positivity from you. Good friends make you feel better about yourself, celebrate your successes, and encourage you to be the best version of yourself. Bad friends can damage your self-esteem and lead to a poor self-image.

Exhibiting positive emotions may make you more lovable. In nearly all cases, showing positive emotions makes one highly relatable, making the person more lovable. Try to reflect on your school days or workplace and note which people you prefer. Showing positive emotions may attract more people around you. There is a high possibility that you prefer a person that shows happiness, hope and is motivated over a gloomy person. Since emotions can be infectious, positive emotions may spur positive feelings from the other person. While positive emotions are desirable, it is counterproductive to bottle up negative emotions in the quest to attract admiration and love. All emotions are necessary and should be expressed. Good relationship etiquette requires that one reads the emotion of the other person. Emotionally intelligence enables one to show requisite levels of empathy.

Emotions and Personal Success

Managed emotions, both positive and negative, can enhance personal success for black women. In this context personal success involves having fruitful social interactions, social relationships, and better financial management. On the positive side, emotions positively affect relationships and personal life management, enhancing personal success. Think of an individual that is motivated, happy, and resilient. The person is likely to also relate well with others.

On the other hand, negative emotions will lead to poor life outcomes. Think of a person that is considered gloomy, temperamental, rigid, and sad. Few people may want to approach and challenge the person to work on their family budget or try a new investment for fear of receiving backlash from the individual. Emotions affect an individual's attitudes towards investment, interacting with others, approachability, and the resilience of the individual. Emotions affect every aspect of life, either directly or indirectly.

Family Factors

From the day we're born, the people around us convey messages that we internalize to form our core belief system about ourselves and the world around us. Therefore, it's no surprise that women with unhealthy role models and less nurturing caretakers would be more prone to developing low self-esteem. Black Women who grow up in environments involving dysfunction, addiction, or abuse tend to be more vulnerable to internalizing feelings of worthlessness. Black Women with parents who are critical toward themselves or others are likely to be highly self-critical. Women whose families conveyed the message that it was not okay to express feelings can develop identity confusion and feelings of wrongdoing that lead to problems with low self-esteem.

Did you experience any of the following things in your family of origin?

- Abuse (physical, emotional, sexual)
- Addiction
- Frequent angry outbursts
- Dysfunction
- Poor communication
- Lack of emotional expression
- Fear of expressing emotion
- Criticism
- Hostile sarcasm
- Unclear expectations

Unfortunately, dysfunction and maladaptive patterns can be passed down for generations. Don't be discouraged if any of these issues are part of your history. By developing an awareness of the problem, you have already taken the first step in breaking that cycle and making lasting improvements.

If you are somebody who grew up with a healthy childhood and marked none of the boxes in the Family Factors exercise, you may find yourself wondering where your low self-esteem could have come from. Know that it's not just women with troubled backgrounds who struggle with low self-esteem.

MOLLY'S STORY

Molly came to see me after being released from the hospital following a suicide attempt. She was a smart, beautiful, and talented high school senior with lots of friends and a bright future. Her caring family was shocked to realize she was struggling with depression and anxiety so severe that she wanted to end her life.

I immediately liked Molly. She was sweet, funny, and, from my eyes, had so much going for her. She had an incredibly supportive family, friends who adored her, and plans to go off to college the following fall. Her main problem was that she was completely unable to see any positives in herself, resulting in poor self-esteem that she didn't think her life was worth living.

It quickly became clear that Molly's standards for herself were quite unrealistic. While she was kind, forgiving, and fair in her expectations and interactions with her many friends and family members, she constantly beat herself up for even the most minor matters. Internally, she judged herself for everything. Every move she made was matched with internal criticism, questioning whether she had said or done something stupid, and hating herself for not being perfect in every endeavor.

Throughout our work together, we began referencing her "different measuring stick"—the one she used to measure herself but that would not make sense for anyone else. When she'd beat herself up for what she saw as "yet another failure," I'd ask her if she'd judge her best friend, sister, or even a stranger in the same manner. Molly began to see the havoc her unfair and faulty ruler created in her life. In time, she was able to interrupt her self-critiques with the image of the faulty ruler. Eventually, she began to consider that imperfection wasn't the end of the world, and just maybe, her life did matter.

Developing and maintaining healthy self-esteem is a process that can take time, yet it is such a worthwhile endeavor for us all. When Molly started maintaining a healthy self-esteem her productivity increased and she even managed to start her own company in 2 years. Imagine how much easier life can be when we simply love and accept ourselves as we are. We can all stand to benefit from building self-esteem in some way. Both men and women can utilize the tools helpful in boosting self-esteem.

However, women face some unique challenges in navigating the nuances of establishing a foundation of self-worth.

Like in *Molly's story*, self-esteem issues can be difficult to readily identify, as they often go hand in hand with other struggles, like depression, anxiety, and anger issues. Low self-esteem can also be masked by substance use, addiction, or even hidden beneath fabricated displays of self-assurance and happiness. The following story encapsulates the experience of a woman who came to therapy for issues of depression and anger management. Still, at the root, she was dealing with very low self-esteem.

Chapter 4: Taoist principles and philosophy

The universe is natural. And according to the Tao, it was neither created nor designed by anyone. Even though there is no personified creator, the Tao is the primal energy that exercises and develops itself, where the original energy becomes the subtle law of its creation. Everything manifested and unmanifested is a miraculous expression of the nature of the Subtle Origin, where no intentional design or manipulation is necessary.

If we indulge in our strong emotions, passions, desires, and ambitions, then the influence of the energy net will be very strong, indeed. If one's energy is light though, the influence of the energy net will also be lighter. Additionally, if an individual leads their life normally and in harmony with the universe, there will be no sign of an energy net at all.

In this world, therefore, each life is responsible only for itself. An individual may also have good fortune when his energy moves to a favorable section of the cycle for them. Great awareness is needed to discern whether a person is really being helped via spiritual growth, or whether they are just responding to the illusion of his religious enthusiasm caused by emotional connectedness or indulgences.

The Key Core Principles of Taoism
The Choice of Spiritualism

Many spiritual endeavors are merely emotional or psychological. And in general, religious rituals are defined as worship. Still, in true honesty, they are either emotional demands or psychological needs which have prevailed since ancient times and are usually steeped in traditional necessity.

Another category of spiritual endeavor might result from your spiritual effort and development; one which is not socially supported. In essence, black women working for personal spiritual development do not come from someone else's charity or kindness. It's a personal endeavor that an individual chooses to do with devoted actioning. Cutting through the issues of the emotions, including the inner psychology, mental conceptions or perceptions, and personal life problems, provides the necessary progression that can help restore your balance and poise as a spiritual being.

In everyday human life, all of us have three spheres. These are the physical, the mental, and the spiritual parts of us. It can't be denied that all life needs material support, and our entire life is not limited to the material sphere only. However, our spirit (or soul) also needs proper development and reflection. The direction of human society has changed radically from the pursuit of the spirit to the pursuit of the material world, or how much we 'have' in terms of financial gain and/or resources.

In today's modern world, the material and mental aspects of life are overemphasized and run from the perception of ego and logic, especially in the form of intellectual knowledge which makes some individuals begin to deny the existence of a spiritual level of life, or the need for soul growth at all.

The Need for Spiritual Growth

People need spiritual growth and development to be whole, but they might assert a 'tunnel vision' view of life due to advances in scientific research and industrial technology. It's true too, that these aspects do not cover the whole scope of human existence as three-part, triune beings. We cannot use the same methods that apply to material discoveries to explore the spiritual sphere, and it would be difficult to do so, for certain. And so, many become disappointed and deny the existence of a spiritual realm at all. These people never really see the error of using the wrong 'tools .' Thus, they move far from the wholeness of life, which can incorporate the spirit as part of one's individualism.

We call the 'journey' or the 'spiritual path' just the common learnings or teachings of basic life. It's also true that modern education mostly pushes aptitude and living on the physical and mental levels, therefore avoiding spiritual matters on the whole. This way of living doesn't support spiritual development, neglecting what some might say is the most essential part of life.

Enhancing Spiritual Development is a Core Need

Spiritual development must deepen and explore the truth for a person to achieve the goal of wholeness and balance, which is done step by step. It takes years for most individuals, and it truly depends on how they receive their spiritual education and work on themself. This is the beginning of individual spiritual development. It's also true that it's a personal matter, so going 'within' is part and parcel of finding answers.

We could say that the body, mind, and spirit should be equally valued and worked upon for true self-cultivation. Gaining spiritual achievement develops from physical essence, with the mind as the major link between the physical and the spiritual spheres. It must organize a harmonious state of enjoyment through a beautiful life. The potential here is everchanging too, and if balance is broken, the scales can be tipped, metaphorically speaking.

In everyday life, very few people are murderers or use violence, but many are emotionally violent. Many people indeed lose their tempers when things don't go their way. And here, the loss of spiritual qualities as virtues, like patience and tolerance (as examples), can make individuals take a violent emotional path. Rather than a more balanced or heart-centered approach, it is the mind (or ego) response to things.

When you are in an eventful circumstance and your mind is not bothered, this is called true peace and true calmness. This occurs when circumstances no longer control the mind, and therefore, it is free. The freedom of the mind is a powerful, purposeful mind, and a very useful mind, indeed.

Stages of the Tao

Stage 1: This occurs when the mind reaches peace and can more easily respond to the subtle and ordinary parts. It is then easy to discern what worldly things are heavier and might disturb your true inner peace, and knowing this can prevent the cause of a downfall.

Stage 2: This stage is when old physical problems clear up by themselves and you no longer need to go to physicians. Your physical body and the mind will feel lighter and happier, too.

Stage 3: At this stage, your vitality is regenerated, and you come back to a state that's more natural and begets a healthier life overall. You'll also begin to follow the right way of living guided by your growing wisdom from within.

Stage 4: Stage 4 occurs after achieving the foundation of the first stages already mentioned. You can live from your heart space (as opposed to the mind/ego) and not be subject to the lower influences that might be more negative, or ego based. You can now connect with the spiritual realm at this stage.

Stage 5: This stage occurs when an individual refines one's physical energy to be higher, with what might be called essential energy. Through perseverance and cultivation, the physical energy is transformed to become chi.

Stage 6: This later stage comes after transforming the gross chi into more subtle chi. After this, you can begin to transform your chi to be more essential, to live as a spiritual being. Spiritual beings can be in the world and remain subtle or not, just as they so wish to be. They are true spirits who have purpose-filled or spiritually guided lives.

Stage 7: This is when the spirit (or soul) is refined and unites completely with the Tao. And now, the ultimate beingness is achieved. This is a true divine path. The individual's light will always respond to lighten the darkness within the world around it, too.

The seven stages to become one with Tao or enjoy complete fulfillment are universal. Any individual who seeks such self-cultivation without seeing these positive results will not achieve Tao.

Strengthening the body's internal energy

All people on the Earth dream of happiness. But not everyone fully understands what happiness is. The concept of happiness is defined by two components: external and internal.

The external component is associated with the conditions and circumstances of human life.

The inner component is connected with the inner world of man. She determines his perception of life, his attitude towards her and the circumstances determining this life.

In the Taoist teachings, happiness is one of the most important, and the ability to be happy, an understanding of what happiness is, is brought up from early childhood. The followers of the Taoist teachings learn to organize and customize their inner world in such a way as to experience a state of happiness, harmony and calm continuously.

And also, master the art of managing circumstances and your destiny. But the most important thing is not only to control the energies, but to increase the body's internal energy. In comprehending the art of being happy, there are secrets for your life to change for the better; you need to comprehend the secrets of feelings and emotions and the paths of movement of energy, that is, energy channels.

Energy channels

Taoists argued that there are two wonderful channels through which energies circulate and these channels have certain points. Most reflex therapists save poor knowledge of the points and their bad feeling. Through the body, you can drive energy through the hand, chest, along any line, but if you go clearly along the meridian, point by point - there is a danger that you will break the natural course of energies.

Working with these wonderful central channels allows you:

 To increase the body's internal energy, so that your energy is activated, you can not only tolerate cold, withstand greater physical exertion without much fatigue, but also develop several supernormal abilities.

 - The central channels serve as the basis, the core for the construction of a stable energy system of the body;

- The central channels serve as a reserve capacity for retaining surplus energy in them, storing them and retrieving them in critical situations.

Exercise: "forking"

So, imagine yourself as a warrior preparing for a decisive attack. First you need to find peace, in many Taoist practices this is also called the cessation of internal dialogue and tune in to battle.

Intensify the brain's work by pressure on the center of the eyebrows. Sit on a stool without a back. The backs of the palms at the same time massage the eyebrows in a circular motion.

Then spend a relaxing movement with two hands along the forehead to the eyes, then down the face, throat to the middle between the nipples of your chest.

In women, the nipples need to be pulled as far as possible, determine the perpendicular to the body, and find this point between the nipples, which is also considered in Taoism as a projection of the center of emotions.

When energy comes to this zone, chest tightness may occur; a massage of this area suppresses it. Periodic massage of this zone, oddly enough, is one of the methods of activating semen in men.

If you learn to use your hands in the right time for you and understand the mechanism and essence of this exercise, you will discover completely different ways of being in this world, you will become a slightly different person.

Exercise: "hammer in stakes"

This exercise is performed immediately after the previous exercise. Continuing to sit, try to "hammer in stakes" by your legs. To do this, hit the heel to stand in the most relaxed position. Imagine raising the patella of your foot and pushing it down so that the leg is at a 90 degree angle, and the heel jerk causes a certain blood supply in the legs.

By the way, a hard push of the heel and walking on the heels make it possible to achieve another goal - to loosen and reduce blood stasis in the anus, a kind of control point for several energy flows. Hard foot massage, shaking, light tapping, jumping on the heels partially eliminate the problem.

Exercise: "revitalizing the body"

Now proceed to the exercise to revitalize the body. To do this, knock a little on the area under the kneecaps. This zone is directly connected with the tendon under which the nerve passes and causes the muscles to contract.

Neurologists often knock on this area to check reflexes. So, after tapping, your energy quickens and goes into the region of the hip joints. When tapping, inhalation should be made at the moment when you intend to strike under the patella and exhale together with the movement of the leg. These breaths should intensify the body's energy.

Exercise: "energy swing"

After you feel the influx of energy, swing forward and lean back so that in a few swings you can relax the two moving zones: the gold and silver bridge. Golden is called the upper body, because the neck is more important, and silver - the lower one.

After relaxing straighten your spine and proceed to turn your head left-right, back and forth, and in a circle clockwise and counterclockwise. In this case, the shoulders should be relaxed, arms relaxed, you can shake them several times and drop your palms down on your knees.

Try to imagine that a kind of dense mass forms inside the palm of your hand, which drains, filling the knee joint. According to Taoist beliefs, this joint is also a repository of souls. When a person dies it is difficult, then souls are released from the knee joints, which are numerous in a person, and not one, as in Christian teaching.

Separate your shoulders breathe easy, without making any effort to maintain balance. After a breath of air, you can leave your head in a position where the back of your head is more flat relative to the energy that is right below, allowing it to flow through you. Sit quietly and breathe, as you are more comfortable and calm. No external sounds should distract you, because any sudden sound can frighten and injure, make the energy freeze in those areas where it has been activated.

To create a guard of breath, throw your arm forward, set mentally the guard who will protect your breath from external encroachments. Repeat the same ejection with the other hand. After that, mentally make a small lock in the throat area, if swallowed, you will have a guard here who will not release excessive energy from the abdomen. A joke, having a share of jokes, everything else is true: the

Taoists have big bellies because they have a lot of energy. Some Taoist practices encourage the development of a lower part for relaxation and then, naturally, for an effort, but nothing should have prevented this inhalation, and the lower abdomen made the inhalation, it was delayed as actively as possible.

Lifestyle And Attitude

Here are some additional clues for living in harmony with the universe—some of which you've seen before, and some completely new:

Spend time in nature. Honor and enjoy the trees, mountains, rivers, and meadows. Take action to protect the environment.

Cultivate playfulness, spontaneity, wonder, and awe. Resurrect your childlike innocence and natural curiosity.

Periodically unplug from your Wi-Fi devices. Shift your focus away from the external screens of your laptop, phone, or tablet and toward the internal screen of your mind. Observe the coming and going of internal thoughts and images. Experiment with visualization practice.

Question the authority of your mind's habitual beliefs, your theories about how things are or how they're supposed to be. Be willing to "try on" a completely different set of beliefs and assumptions just for fun.

Have a sense of humor.

Appreciate subtlety and mystery.

Celebrate Taoist art forms such as poetry, painting, and calligraphy.

Appreciate simplicity. Fully enjoy and satisfy what you have already, what's here right now. Downsize. Eliminate physical and mental clutter, allowing space for something new to appear or for the space itself to become more vibrant.

This doesn't mean that you can't own and enjoy material things: houses, cars, fancy shoes, mountain bikes, *etc.* Just don't rely on them for true and lasting happiness—a task they simply were not designed to accomplish.

Chapter 5: Why mindfulness is important but not enough

Mindfulness and meditation

As emotional beings, we are naturally mindful. Still, it can be difficult to be fully present in our lives when we are dealing with high anxiety or anger or other negative emotions. When we practice mindfulness, we force ourselves to face these emotions, consider them and learn to understand them. We can cultivate mindfulness through various techniques, the most common and widely practiced being meditation.

Meditation is an excellent relaxation technique that helps us connect with our inner truths. The goal of meditation is to quiet the mind and body, remove insignificant thoughts, and develop inner balance by interacting with our emotional selves without the constant external and internal chatter. Meditation is a rather simple activity, but calming the body and mind is easier said than done. By introducing meditation into your routine, you will get better and better at it, and you will begin to crave the positive and peaceful feelings it can bring out.

When we meditate, we steer our awareness away from the external and turn it inwards, paying attention to what the body and mind are doing without the external noise of life.

Meditation promotes relaxation, which relieves the body of stress and stress hormones and allows it to function more easily. When the body is less stressed, there are fewer physical distractions from what is going on in the mind. When we are meditating, we are naturally more aware of our thoughts and emotions, and we are open to the insights we have within ourselves.

How Black Women Can Use Mindfulness to Recognize their Emotional Triggers

For the most part, our intense negative emotions manifest automatically due to some internal or external trigger. This could be a negative thought, a traumatic event, or even an unexpected change. What triggers emotions in you will not necessarily trigger others, and what triggers emotions in others may not do the same for you. This is where mindfulness comes in. When you find yourself caught by the tide of negative emotion, try to identify what exactly caused you to feel this way. Here's a list of some possible triggers for common negative emotions:

Anger

Betrayal by a trusted person or entity

Being disrespected, challenged, or insulted

Being physically or emotionally threatened

Being patronized or condescended to

Being lied to/given misinformation

The injustice done to you or others

Discrimination/prejudice

Fear

Threat of death

Threat of injury or pain

Loss of perceived safety/security

Dark or unfamiliar environment

Imagining a threatening event

Reliving past fear or trauma

Feeling exposed/vulnerable

Anxiety

Anticipating failure or discomfort

Feeling unprepared or insecure

Feeling inadequate or worthless

Negative self-talk/self-deprecation

Upcoming event, performance, or challenge

Social and/or familial conflict

Remembering bad experiences

Personal strain (due to finances, travel, etc.)

Sadness/Grief

Major illness in a friend or loved one

The death of a friend or loved one

Temporary separation from loved ones

Feeling rejected or unwanted

A loss of identity or self-worth

Anticipating future tragedy

Disappointment in self or others

Involuntary memories of loss or disappointment

Once we know what is triggering our emotional distress, we can begin to put together techniques and strategies to cope with it healthily.

When you can identify what is causing your emotional turmoil and have the self-awareness to recognize your responses, you are better prepared to try coping strategies and allow them to work. Coping with intense emotions is difficult when one does not understand what (s)he is feeling and why. Practice mindfulness to get to know your emotional self.

How Black Women Can Create Inner Peace

Inner peace is a thing we hear about often, but may feel is outside of our reach. Many people talk about it, and seek it out, never knowing that the search itself may be the very thing that is keeping them from attaining it. Trying so hard to control the external world to gain inner peace seems common, yet it is counterproductive and only creates more turmoil. The first step black women can create inner peace is letting go. There are several other elements to help one obtain peacefulness, but letting go is foremost. Creating inner peace is mostly an understanding between yourself and the world that you are who you are, and the world is not in control. Everything that occurs outside of you only interferes with your inner peace when you allow it to by reacting to it.

That's right; you control your inner peace with reacting to what happens in your life and the world around you. Although this focus is introspection, one cannot leave things unresolved from a time when inner peace was not a priority. Things from the past that may still be a source of turmoil for you must be put to rest. Having things unfinished will feel that way until you finish them.

They will continue to interfere in your journey to mindfulness and need to be resolved.

Apologize to whomever you know you should. Make amends with whomever you can, even if it's only for the sake of your inner peace. Tie up the loose ends that you may have left at schools, old workplaces, old living situations, and any other relationship of any kind. Most importantly, forgive everyone. Once you have forgiven, you take away any power those issues have over you. It is empowering and freeing to let them know you have forgiven them, in any way you are able. It helps everyone involved, and you can mark that off your list forever. Resolve each of the open-ended contentions, and settle up all of your affairs. This will ease you into acceptance.

Letting things go will become easier the more you do it, and you have already practiced surrender and acceptance by resolving lingering matters. Now you can take it a step further by accepting all things that you cannot change completely, and surrendering to what is. This does not mean to throw your hands up in the air and give up. There is a finesse required to keep from crossing the line between accepting and just checking out. Acknowledgement is the key to acceptance. You must first let yourself be aware of what you cannot change to surrender and truly accept them.

An example of this could be spilled milk. You can ignore it, and decide not to let it affect you, but it eventually will become a rotten, stinky mess. When you notice the spilled milk, accept that it was spilled, and surrender to the fact that you must clean it up and move on; you eliminate spilled milk disrupting your peace and keep yourself from a more difficult and cruel problem in the future.

Mindfulness: How to Meditate

Meditation is arguably one of the most amazing and effective practices to help you achieve mindfulness, peace, happiness, and prosperity. This practice helps you better understand yourself and your sense of purpose in life by silencing your racing mind so you can focus better on your thoughts and better understand how they influence you.

When you gain insight into your thoughts and mind, you become aware of yourself and as your self-awareness improves, understanding others becomes easier. This slowly helps you build and then improve your EQ.

Here's how black women can meditate to achieve all these goals:

Choose an ideal meditation time. Make sure the time you pick is a time you are free so you don't constantly feel distracted while you meditate. Try to stick to this particular time regularly so you become consistent in the practice.

Next, pick a peaceful meditation spot and ensure the area is free from distracting persons or objects. Declutter, clean, and organize the area. Clutter is a big distraction and you must declutter your meditation spot.

Before you meditate, wear something comfortable and sit down in a comfortable pose. You can cross your legs, kneel, sit on a chair, or even lie down.

Set a timer for 2 to 5 minutes; it is best to stick to 2 minutes to start so you do not overwhelm yourself.

Close your eyes and think of any peaceful or happy memory to relax.

Once you feel calmer, slowly bring all your attention to your breath. Your job right now is to stay with your breath throughout your meditation session, and this helps improve your focus. In time, you'll easily focus on one thing at a time and you'll find it very easy to concentrate on different emotions and the thoughts that trigger those emotions to explore better and understand yourself.

Coming back to your breath, pay attention to your in-breath as you inhale through your nose and then with your out-breath as you exhale through your mouth. While you inhale and exhale, focus on how this practice makes you feel. Notice the different sensations you experience as you respire such as the fluttering feeling in your abdomen, rising and falling of your belly, *etc.*

As you focus on these sensations and the movements in your body as you breathe, concentrate so that you don't wander off in thought. However, if you still find your thoughts straying, gently acknowledge that thinking has taken place and then very calmly nudge your thoughts back to your breath. You can do that by counting your breath.

Keep doing so throughout your session.

Write down how you felt in your journal as you end your practice. Do you feel calmer? Do you feel less stressed and anxious now? Write down the answers to these questions because they will help you figure out how well you did.

Follow these steps to meditate daily and soon you'll nurture the habit of meditating. Once you can easily concentrate on your breath for five minutes, increase the duration of your meditative practice and do it more often in the day. By doing this, your level of focus and calmness will strengthen.

When you achieve this, use meditation to focus on your thoughts to explore and understand them. To do that, take any one thought or emotion and explore its essence. Explore it to understand why you feel that way, the first time you felt that way, and what triggered that emotion or thought. For instance, if you feel frustrated, think of the first time you felt extremely agitated and strengthened that emotion.

When you start understanding your thought process, ask yourself questions such as

"What do I want in life?"

"Does my life have a purpose?"

"Is there any goal that I am motivated to achieve?"

"What brings meaning to my life?"

"How can I improve my quality of life?"

"How can I feel good about myself?"

Explore these questions and other similar questions and you'll soon start becoming more aware of your emotions, feelings, and needs. Make sure you write everything down in a journal to work on those things later.

With time, your level of mindfulness will increase. You'll start to stay mindful of yourself while engaged in your routine work. This will help you pinpoint a certain emotion as it develops to work on it instantly.

For instance, if you talk to someone and start losing confidence, you'll quickly become aware of that. Instead of letting your confidence grow weaker, you'll excuse yourself from your listener and will work to find the root cause of the problem. This shall help you take charge of your emotions and situation and save yourself from making a fool of yourself.

Mindfulness for a Toxic Environment

When you feel trapped in a toxic environment but you can't immediately get out of the situation or the office if it's affecting the entire office, you can do some things to stop the negativity from impacting you and your health. When you have to work in a toxic environment or with toxic people you can:

Take a step back. Breathe deeply and remind yourself that you are not the problem and you can choose not to let that negativity affect you.

Visualize that negativity rolling off you the way that water rolls off you during a shower. You may not avoid the negativity shower but you can choose to let it all go down the drain instead of clinging to you.

Create a positivity oasis for yourself. If you have an office, a cubicle, or private space, create a soothing oasis just for you. Hang up art that you find soothing and positive. Write positive messages to yourself on sticky notes and hang them up. Keep a plant or flowers in there to reconnect with nature.

Making Time for Yourself

When you are juggling work and a relationship and family obligations it can seem like there's never any time for yourself. But you have to make your self-care a priority, including making time for mindfulness.

Carving out a few minutes for yourself each day can change the quality of your life forever. You will be healthier, happier, less anxious and less stressed out all the time. Your relationships with everyone around you, including yourself, will improve.

If you have a schedule packed with responsibilities you may need to get creative about finding time to meditate. This list of ways to fit some meditation time into your day is filled with tips from real people who have found clever ways to take care of everyone else and take care of themselves too:

Get up 30 minutes early. You might hate losing the sleep, but the benefits of meditation will make up for the sleep.

Turn off the TV an hour earlier at night. Are you watching that show or just listening to it in the background? Turn it off and meditate.

Turn off your tablet, computer and smartphone. If you are checking emails and surfing the Web before bed, you have to meditate. Facebook can wait, but your self-care can't. Turn it off and meditate.

Make lunches the night before. The 20 minutes you spend making lunches in the morning could be time to mediate. Make all the lunches the night before and have them ready to go in the morning.

Make breakfast in the slow cooker. There will be a hot meal waiting when you get up and you will have 15 minutes that you can use to meditate. Slow cooked oats in the slow cooker are delicious and healthy.

Make meals ahead of time. Once a week cook up some casseroles or other dinners, and freeze them so that you can just pull out a healthy dinner during the week when you are busy. You can use the time while it's cooking to meditate.

Take more baths. Baths are a great place to meditate because it's quiet time when no one else will bother you. Or, if you don't have time for a bath meditate in the shower. Stand under the hot water and be present. It will refresh your mind and your body.

Leave for work 10 minutes earlier. You can sneak in a quick meditation in your car before you go into the office, and it's a good way to start the day focused and ready to work.

Skip practices. You don't need to watch every sports practice or activity your child does. While your child is busy head back to the car to get a little Mindful Meditation time. It will help you release all the stress of the day so that you can focus on your family at night.

Go for a walk. Meditation doesn't have to be done sitting down and being perfectly still. Leave the MP3 player at home and go for a walk in your neighborhood, even if it's just around the block. Breathe in the fresh air and notice the beautiful world around you.

You will find a further deepening on meditation below, including various meditation types and practices. Black spirit is peaceful, sympathetic, tribal, which is why it has many points in common with oriental philosophy and relaxation techniques. The sections of these two manuscripts in one, especially those dedicated to meditation and Taoist philosophy, have precisely the aim of highlighting these common characteristics and encouraging the reader, especially if a black woman (but not only), to reconnect with her own spirituality

Chapter 6: Self-esteem

Healthy Self-Esteem

Generally speaking, black women with healthy self-esteem see themselves as worthwhile and capable. They have an accurate view of themselves and feel secure, even while facing challenges or setbacks. They can recognize and appreciate their strengths and accept their shortcomings, realizing that flaws and weaknesses are an inevitable part of life. Black women with healthy self-esteem set healthy goals and feel deserving and capable of good. They respect themselves and engage in healthy behaviors.

Healthy self-esteem comes with an understanding that your value is not determined by perfection or accomplishments, and that worth does not have to be proven or earned. Rather, self-worth is a given, and it comes from within, from a deep personal belief that you are fundamentally good. It does not involve getting caught up in seeking worth through external sources or gaining reassurance through the approval, validation, or attention.

Self-esteem is defined as the realistic appreciation of one's self. If you want to increase your self-esteem, you can establish certain steps in your routine to help yourself.

The Link Between Self-Control and Self-Esteem

Self-control isn't just linked to happiness, it's been linked to increased levels of self-esteem too.

Each time, show the ability to exercise self-control over any aspect of your life, your self-esteem and belief in yourself will be the one that reaps the benefits.

When you see the result of just how much you accomplished because you persisted despite how you were feeling, your self-esteem is given a boost, along with the belief in yourself, which eventually boosts your happiness along with it.

It reinforces in your mind that you are capable of doing this.

Every achievement that you make through self-control will boost your happiness and self-esteem just a little more and fuel the desire to keep going, going and going.

This desire will keep fueling you forward until eventually before you know it, you're on a roll and you've become an unstoppable force.

Factors that Influence Self-Esteem

Self-esteem is something that develops over time. When you are young, self-esteem is something satisfied externally. People like friends at school, siblings, parents, and other relatives you are

94

close to play a major role in how you feel about yourself. When they give positive feedback, it helps build self-esteem. Likewise, how they treat you influences how you feel about your impact in the world.

One of the reasons that black women struggle with self-esteem is because they were not given positive support and reinforcement that they needed to know their worthiness in the world. Children with low self-esteem only continue to struggle as teenagers. Even if they are approved their peers, they still might struggle with the judgment or criticism from their parents. Many factors influence self-esteem once you are an adult. This includes:

- Your perception of others
- How others see you
- The way that you think about others
- Experience at work or in school
- Presence of disability or illness
- Religious or cultural traditions

Within these different factors, you have the most control over are your thoughts and your position. You'll notice that many of the strategies for growing your self-esteem focus on changing your thoughts and the way you see the world around you. This allows change to happen from the inside out.

How black women can Increase their Self-Esteem

Re-affirm your positive traits. Just as we often think negative things about ourselves, we must also learn to affirm positive traits. For example, maybe you're constantly telling yourself, "You're a lazy person." You've been telling yourself that for so long that you are believing it and you've internalized that voice. To see yourself positively and improve your self-esteem, try telling yourself the opposite. Tell yourself that you're a good friend, a good daughter, a kind person, or a generous person.

Avoid comparisons. One of the toughest parts of developing your self-esteem is realizing that you cannot compare yourself to others. Too often, we compare ourselves with people around us like family, co-workers, friends, or people we don't even know thanks to the exposure to social media. Whether it's about looks, money, personal possessions or whatever it may be, the trap of comparing is that you never feel good enough.

Focus on self-care. Whether you are exercising, treating yourself to a spa day, or getting a good night's sleep, it's important that you physically take care of yourself to your mental health. Exercise is proven to release serotonin, a neurotransmitter of the brain that creates happiness and contentment. Whether it's an hour at the gym or just going for an evening walk before dinner, take some time to exercise so you are physically taking care of yourself.

Help others. Studies show that helping someone else or volunteering can help you feel better about yourself. It takes you out of your mindset and urges you to think about someone else. The best way to increase your feelings of self-worth is volunteering face-to-face, such as at a homeless shelter or a soup kitchen. But if you can also donate money or provide services online, you can also increase your self-worth. You can feel like you are part of a cause and helping people. You have a purpose. This gives value to you and your time, and you feel part of a greater community. This increases your self-worth and self-esteem and how you feel about yourself.

Remind yourself that you are not your circumstances. Tell yourself repeatedly that even if you are going through a tough time right now, you may not be soon. Circumstances occur in our life that is sometimes out of our control. As the saying goes, "this, too, shall pass." With hard work, compassion, and patience, whatever tough time you are going through will soon ease itself.

Why do Black Women Suffer Poor Self Image?

Self-esteem is fundamental to identity, and a critical ingredient in anyone's feeling genuine happiness. It helps us feel validated from within, but sometimes, despite having a strong resolve, this self-worth can be toppled by external forces. Black women are especially susceptible to this as the media and society control what is "acceptable", particularly in terms of appearance, behavior, and societal roles.

The Body Question for Black Women

Body image is all about how we see our physical selves. A distorted body image is an unrealistic perception of one's own body. The official term is body dysmorphia, and we all have it to some degree. For most black women, it's a simple an easy thing to manage with a little rationality and common sense. Growing comfortable in your skin also very much comes with maturity.

Much like overall self-esteem in general, negative body image can stem from childhood experiences and an unhealthy comparison with the rest of society later in life. Of course friends and family also play a role here.

Like problems with low self-esteem, a negative body image isn't something to be solved by sweeping it under the rug. For proper recovery to take place, it's important to recognize the problem to begin with. To acknowledge the negative feelings that you are currently dealing with. To discover how to make your body feel comfortable, while eradicating the irrational thoughts of not being enough.

Movement and dance therapy are great alternative methods to improve one's body image. They can be used as a tool to help build trust and appreciate your body through creative expression and experimentation. It will feel strange and uncomfortable at first, but I have seen many black women flower once a small degree of competence is achieved. It's a liberating practice with so many confidence building and health related benefits.

Connection with Your Body

We are all different and should be encouraged to embrace these differences. Often we can't help but aspire to these ideals, to have that perfect physique or face, too resemble that actress or TV presenter.

We intuitively know that it's really what's on the inside that matters. Our physical bodies shouldn't have to be a determining factor of our worth, nor should it overbearingly affect the way we feel about ourselves. However, this is a difficult concept to grasp for most, especially those who already have a poor self-image. More often than not, they are already dealing with feelings of self-hate and worthlessness, and they may well be on their way to triggering depression or developing an eating disorder in extreme cases.

In this sense, a negative self-image will have a huge impact on relationships, no matter what kind. It will affect how we feel and interact with others on every level. This almost always puts undue pressure on couples. In a romantic relationship, the partner of someone who has a negative self-image will usually offer words of encouragement to counter the negativity, hoping to solve the problem. Although, even the most well-intentioned words and honest compliments will fall on deaf ears to those with a poor self-image. This will spark additional tensions and inevitably cause the relationship suffer.

It can also affect a couple's intimacy. Someone who doesn't feel satisfied about how they look, will typically struggle with intimacy. Feelings of unattractiveness and low self-confidence will cause them to second-guess their partner's feelings and attraction towards them. They may feel uncomfortable being touched or being naked in front of them.

Suppose you feel that you are dealing with poor self-image, and you notice that it's already affecting your relationships and life in general. In that case, you should consider having a self-image makeover. Here are some of the things you can do to achieve this, albeit slowly:

Choose to see your accomplishments

Dwelling on your outer appearance all the time isn't going to do you any good. You don't look like anybody else, and if you keep comparing yourself to those around you, there will always be moments when you will fall short. Instead of nitpicking all your physical flaws, channel your energy into reminding yourself of what you're good at.

Say no to negative self-talk

Black Women can be extremely critical of themselves; somehow, it's easy for us to see our flaws when we look in the mirror. While we already know that no one is perfect and that there will always be details we wish we could change about ourselves, the ability to accept oneself wholly truly sets the happy people apart from those who have a negative self-image.

This isn't going to be an overnight change of course. The transition from negative to positive thinking can take some time, so you have to be patient with yourself. Keep those negative thoughts at bay, and do a little more each day to build that snowball of positive self-image bit-by-bit.

Take baby steps

If you are dissatisfied with your physical appearance to the point that even shifting your thoughts isn't working, your list of viable solutions for achieving happiness will become shorter. You can try harder and be more patient when fully accepting yourself, or you can do something to change what you dislike about your body by focusing on one small change at a time.

Instead of signing up for the gym, dance class and new diet plan all in one go. Knock each off one month at a time. Start with just 30 minutes of exercise per day for the first month, walking, cycling, swimming, *etc.* Then add in that Pilates class once a week the following month. Once these activities are fully rocking, start improving your diet with cleaner carbohydrates and reduced sugar meals. Taking on these tasks one at a time makes them exponentially easier to achieve, and more critically more sustainable in the long term.

Open yourself up to others

This will be the most difficult for black women, but if you want to stop viewing yourself in such a negative light, you need to start letting the people around you know how you truly feel. This is required all the more if you are in a committed relationship. Your significant other shouldn't be kept in the dark about the anxieties you feel regarding your self-image. You need to open up to them, and in doing so, they'll better understand what you're going through, as well as the reasons for your actions and behaviors. The more they know, the more they'll be able to figure out a way to help you get through your troubles.

Sometimes, even the support of loved ones may fall short in talking you out of your negative self-image. It might be best to talk to a counselor about your feelings in such instances. A professional's opinions can help you gain a better perspective of your situation and teach you how to manage your negative thoughts. They will help you understand what triggers your poor self-image, and lead you to solutions that can greatly improve how you see yourself.

These seemingly small steps can be the change you need to make a big difference in getting your happiness back on track. The key is to integrate small changes into your life little by little in ways that are not overwhelming, but will help you gain a healthier disposition each day. Regaining a more healthy self-image is a marathon not a sprint. Making just a 1% improvement each week will compound into a huge improvement in no time at all.

Social Media and Self-Image for black women

Social media updates us on what's going on in the world, keeps us connected with family and friends in other parts of the country, provides us with entertainment, and helps our businesses grow, but it also has some drawbacks.

Many black women now turn to social media for advice, support, connection, and distraction. Spending too much time on social media can increase anxiety because of the sheer volume of information and opinions. Even though we know social media illustrates only a curated snapshot of an individual's life, it is human nature to compare. When black women compare themselves to other women, this can decrease self-confidence and an increase in self-doubt. Likewise, following Instagram celebrities and influencers can also lead to the comparison trap and reinforce feelings of being less-than.

When black women use social media to distract themselves from and avoid the real world, it generally leads to perpetuating the feelings they were seeking to avoid in the first place—self-doubt, shame, and guilt.

Negative Effects of Friends on Your Self-esteem

Here are a few different ways that friends can influence black women's self-esteem negatively:

Your friends can cause a sensational decrease of your self-esteem: People who feel sub-par compared to others generally continue contrasting themselves with them and they attempt to discover issues with themselves. These sorts of friends influence your self-esteem since they repeatedly dissect you for the same number of potential imperfections as they can discover. These friends may offer negative remarks about something you did, and there is a genuine loss of your self-esteem. Nonetheless, your self-esteem would not be influenced when you comprehend that their reasoning examples bring about the issue.

Some friends may put down all that you endeavor to do, particularly those that they never figured out how to do. Try not to think little of the impact of such programming at the forefront of your thoughts. The proceeds with reiteration of an announcement can transform deceptions into a strong conviction.

Your friends restricting convictions can contaminate you. One of the most remarkable ways, friends adversely influence your self-esteem is by moving their constraining convictions to you. They will attempt to persuade you that their deceptions are right and you will probably trust them if your feelings are not sufficiently able to check their impact.

At the point when somebody begins to put you down, the most ideal approach to keep anybody from influencing your self-esteem is to go up against them strongly to invalidate their announcements as not being upheld by the verifiable proof. Try not to withdraw, strongly express that they should acknowledge that you do not concur with them. At that point continue to refute them by succeeding.

How Black Women Can Use Positive Thinking to Build Confidence and Self-Esteem

When you think positively, it stays with you for several minutes. However, research shows that when you use that positive attitude to develop resources and build skills, it increases your ability to learn. Take the example of a child who is playing outside. They may be running around a field or swinging on a vine (physical skills) while playing with friends (social skills). Additionally, their observation and exploration of the world around them engage their creative skills. As running around, exploring, and playing with friends are enjoyable, the positive emotions make it more likely that the child will continue building their physical, social, and creative skills by playing outside. Even once that child has gone off to college, their athletic skills might earn them a scholarship or a place playing professional sports, while their social skills may give them the option to work closely with a team of people or run a business. Even though the skills remain, the person might not feel those initial positive feelings that helped them learn the skill. By contrast, negative emotions have the opposite effect. When you are experiencing negative emotions like those you would feel when in danger, your mind is only focused on what is happening at that immediate time. This means you cannot focus on building skills that will benefit you in the future.

How Black Women Overcoming Self-Doubt

Self-esteem begins and ends with how much you trust yourself. If you believe in yourself as a person, as someone who is fundamentally good, as someone who can get things done, and as someone who is not dependent upon the approval or others, you are probably high on the self-esteem scale. Conversely, if you doubt your capabilities and competencies, if you are never quite sure of how good a job you've done, you are pulling down your self-esteem. Overcoming self-doubt requires building self-esteem.

Believe in yourself, set the bar high, and do not let anyone else be your judge. Of course, it's important to acknowledge criticism, since we all can learn to do better, but as long as you have met your own standard of excellence, you may feel a sense of pride and accomplishment, and your self-esteem and self-confidence will be strong.

How to become familiar with one's dark side

We are used to talking about toxic people and the toxicity of relationships and environments, but very often it is not easy to define this type of behavior. Toxic and negative people are people who engage in behaviors aimed at manipulating others and victimizing themselves, lacking any form of empathy.

Toxic and negative people are not people who are sad or who are going through a difficult time, but they are people who dump their problems on others, or do not take into consideration the needs and rights of others. According to some scholars, both psychologists and sociologists, our age is characterized by a high dose of toxicity, due to the uncertainties and instability of daily life, which are very often joined by alienating relationships both at work and in the family and among affections.

For example, work can be an environment in which toxic relationships are easily created, especially in those environments where the rule of productivity and competition between colleagues prevails to achieve specific goals, which can lead to the emergence of rivalry, envy, low self-esteem and frustration by creating an unhealthy work system that threatens the well-being of the organization itself.

But toxic relationships can also affect the family and relationships between parents, children and brothers or sisters. In this case the damage that such relationships can create are perhaps even stronger and deeper because they can last over the years, and very often it is not easy to just move away from the relationship but it is also important to rebuild one's self-knowledge through a therapeutic path.

Toxic people are also harmful to health

Toxic relationships are bad not only from an emotional point of view, but also from a physical point of view: exposure to toxic behaviors weakens our health and our brain.

But how do you understand what toxic behaviors are and learn how to manage them? The first step in recognizing toxic behaviors is to understand that all toxic behaviors are illogical, because they are all behaviors that tend to spread malaise and manipulation without leading to a resolution of the situation.

This awareness can help us understand if the situation we are experiencing has logical and balanced dynamics or if it is the result of illogical and meaningless dynamics. Unfortunately, it is not always easy to recognize a toxic relationship, due to learned behavioral patterns or past traumas or personal characteristics, such as low self-esteem, which do not allow to recognize the differences between the dynamics of a healthy and a toxic relationship.

How to limit or remove toxic people

Limiting or removing toxic people is not as obvious as it seems, because very often they are people we love. It is important to learn to recognize toxic behaviors, to implement defensive strategies that help us not to succumb to the heaviness of these attitudes.

Cognitive empathy and emotions

Meeting a negative, manipulative, or victimizing person will likely bring you a lot of stress and confusion - you will need a good dose of emotional intelligence and cognitive empathy to deal with it. In this sense, it will be important to be able to manage emotions better and not get too involved, so as not to fall back into the patterns that the toxic person is putting in place. This is why we also talk about cognitive empathy: as a method to understand the mechanisms underlying the reasoning of the person in front of us, without letting ourselves be carried away by emotions, to understand what is happening and what are the dynamics and motivations that trigger in this person his negativity.

Assertiveness

Negative people always try to complicate things, to argue and manipulate reality, provoking the interlocutor to get his attention. It is important not to give in to provocation, or to ignore it even by changing the topic of the conversation. In this way we will demonstrate that what for him is a deep offense or a problem, does not matter to us, to the point of minimizing or ignoring it, bringing the conversation back to a more rational and serene level.

Don't get involved

Do not fall into the trap of provocation by the toxic person who will try to highlight all your flaws to make your self-esteem plummet. On the contrary, try to be convinced of your ideas and not to respond with insults. Normally the attacker is the first to have problems. Do not get caught up in the vortex of guilt, but try to explain to the victim or pessimistic person what things really are, letting him know that it is not the world that is angry with him, but his actions that shape reality and that however you are not guilty of what is happening to him.

Set limits

Setting your own limits is important not to get overwhelmed. For example, if the person does not listen to you, ask them to respect the dialogue and listen to you until the end. Learn to say no to situations or relationships that you don't want to keep because they hurt you. Not all people have to be part of your life.

Be compassionate

Although toxic people are negative and heavygoing people, very often they are like that because they are going through a bad time or because they feel weak and vulnerable. In the face of their aggressions, it is useful to gloss over and try to understand them. This does not mean getting absorbed by their demons, but trying to explain to them what they are doing and why and that they are not respecting us. If they do not understand it, moving away from these people may be the solution, but in many cases, when they are close to us it is not possible. This is why trying to communicate is important, perhaps even recommending a therapeutic path.

How Black Women Can Heal their Inner Child

The Black female is assaulted in her tender years by all those common forces of nature at the same time that she is caught in the tripartite crossfire of masculine prejudice, white illogical hate, and Black lack of power.

Specifically, the significant healing that can occur when we create space within our lives to acknowledge compassionately that this aspect of ourselves exists. To some, the idea of reconnecting to one's inner child may sound foreign and odd. I think that's fair. For many Black women, the ability to embrace our inner child is problematic because, as little Black girls, many of us were not able to exist in a childlike state. As a result, the idea of connecting to our innocence and vulnerability can feel scary and, for some, unsafe. However, for true metamorphosis and alignment to occur, we must be willing to heal at all levels of ourselves.

It is a psychological reality that is a crucial aspect of the woman you are today and the congruent woman that you are becoming.

While the depth and breadth of inner child work can look different for everyone, its relevance to the work completed in the phase of ego confrontation is crucial. Many of the behavioral, emotional, and relationship difficulties that we experience in adulthood today stem from childhood interpretations.

On the other hand, if you were reprimanded continuously as a child, you would grow up adopting and applying that language to yourself any time you made a mistake. This is also an applicable explanation for those of you who grew up without one or both of your biological parents. While you may not have been told that you were terrible, the mere absence of your parents seeded this belief. Please note that the example I have shared here is pretty straightforward.

When our inner child is blocked, we are robbed of our natural spontaneity and zest for life. When our inner child is hidden, so are we. These are just some of the examples that indicate that your wounded inner child is operating in your life.

First, one has to become conscious of their inner child. Remaining unconscious is what empowers this version of self to hop into the driver's seat of your life. This process entails naming the pain from your earlier years and the coinciding emotions and beliefs that accompanied them.

Second, because the pain that we are holding and how we are holding it isn't always evident, you must be willing to examine how your coping strategies are attached to it. Trauma, disappointment, and loss that go unnamed become stored unknowns—harbored in the heart, the mind, and the body. Take a few moments to breathe and connect with yourself.

Tips on how to black women can build Self-Confidence

Being confident in yourself actually means nothing than knowing your capabilities and worth. The more you work on your emotional intelligence and develop your EQ you will feel much more confident. However, here are a couple of starting tips you can use:

Identify your weaknesses

The first step in the journey of becoming self-confident is becoming aware of the self. The foremost task for anyone who wants to become self-confident is to identify his weaknesses. These are areas of your life that make you unsure of yourself. It can be your personality trait or a physical trait. Always remember there is no such weakness that one cannot overcome. All it takes is hard work and dedication.

Accept Who You Are

What it literally comes down to is that everyone is unique. However, you should become aware that that is an excellent thing. There is no need to worry about the things that you are not good at. Instead of that, a much better way is to accept who you are and look for ways to improve. For instance, you can always learn a new skill by applying to a class in your community.

Plan out your course of action

Set aside a fixed amount of time from your daily schedule where you will single-mindedly addresses your concerns. If it is losing weight then you will exercise for that period of time not concerning yourself with other mortal affairs of this life. Set yourself realistic and manageable targets that you can foresee yourself achieving in a relatively short time span. Most people do not even initiate this change required to gain self-confidence.

Act upon it

Having once identified your weaknesses, it becomes the time to act upon them. You must not be hesitant of a lifestyle change or a mental makeover because once you decide to overcome your weaknesses, your life will change for certain. Most people remain snugly wrapped up in the cocoon of their comfort zones and don't want to step out and sweat it out. It is essential to remember that you will have to endure much in order to change the way you are.

Reward yourself

Rewards are an imperative to work harder and with more dedication. Unless you reward yourself along with your journey of transformation, the journey will appear too arduous to complete. Rewards in no way mean stepping out of the line and deviating yourself from your goal but just a little token of pampering. This little reward gives you further motivation and keeps you going. This is to show that you love yourself and appreciate all the efforts that you are making in order to induce a lifestyle change.

Building Your Self-Confidence

Knowing what self-confidence is, and what attributes it possesses, is essential to establishing a goal to aim for in the quest for self-esteem and self-confidence. This understanding is the foundation of learning how to assess and build one's level of self-esteem, reaching a place where you feel you are the master of your own destiny.

Acknowledge Your Successes

One of the reasons that people have confidence issues is because they focus on things they are struggling with. Instead of that, try thinking of all the right things you have done in the last couple of days. Celebrate the little successes, such as managing to complete the task at work before the deadline. Don't accept the positive stuff as a routine. Acknowledge them and stop for a second (or longer if needed) to celebrate them. The point is that you are doing a bunch of great things and you should know that.

Don't Compare Yourself to Others

This one is related to the first tip in this subsection. Never compare your life to someone else's because we all have unique life paths and that's the beauty of it. Trust me; you can never win when you compare yourself to others. Instead, try this – compare yourself to the version of yourself from a couple of months or years ago. What changed? What other changes you can make?

List Things You Like About Yourself

When you have a bit of time with yourself, try listing a couple of good things that you did during the day or simply the traits you like about yourself. It doesn't have to take long; two minutes is enough to think and acknowledge those things. It can be anything from "I am thoughtful to our dog because I feed him every morning" to "I am a funny person, and I can always make my friends laugh." Taking a couple of seconds to acknowledge those things will make you feel better and make you realize your worth.

Chapter 7: Practical Techniques Black Women Can use to Manage Emotions

Deep Breathing

Negative emotions have invaded our life to the extent of threatening every part of our being. Cases of anxiety, stress, frustrations, and other negative emotions are nowadays rampant in black womens' lives. As a result, they are prompting them to look for a formidable solution that will help us deal with it. Fortunately, deep breathing and mindfulness prove to be part and parcel of this great solution. Mindfulness, on the other hand, refers to the ability to realize your presence.

When you are experiencing a huge bout of stress, anger or frustration, it feels difficult to manage those emotions and think sanely. Fortunately, a good fix to this problem lies in simply learning to calm down and taking deep, slow breaths.

Pay more attention to your feelings and emotions and be on the lookout for signs of stress. If you find yourself exasperating, gasping for breath, and pacing back and forth, sit down and take deep breaths.

Inhale deeply through your nose to a count of four, five, or six, and hold that breath in for the same count. Slowly exhale it through your mouth to a count slightly longer than the one you inhaled on so if you inhaled to a count of five, exhale to a count of seven or eight. When you feel angry, scared or stressed out, inhale more to release that built-up frustration and exhale deeply. Take about 10 breaths using this technique and imagine all your built-in negativity moving out of your system. You will feel calmer within a few minutes.

Every time you feel a powerful emotion stir inside you, take deep breaths, and disengage yourself from that storm of emotions by doing something relaxing. For example, if earlier you were talking to your best friend and had an argument that angered you, excuse yourself from the situation, breathe deeply, and then do something relaxing such as taking a stroll in a park, drink something cool, or watch a funny video.

Work on this strategy every time you find negativity looming over you and within a little while, you will feel calmer and more emotionally stable than before.

There are several ways you can use to bring back your mind into your realities, as shown below.

You need to find a relaxed and comfortable position always before starting the mindfulness breathing.

Take a more exceptional look at your body then relax it

You can then tune into your breath

You must be kind to your roaming mind

Your meditation should be a maximum of 5 to 7 minutes

Lastly, you must do check-ups. That is, checking in before checking out.

Exercise to Manage Any Emotion

• Start by closing your eyes and invoke your attention inwardly.

• Rather than trying to escape the emotion, accommodate it. Try to observe it as if it is not yours akin to a scientist examining a new specimen.

• Interrogate yourself and determine why the emotion is in your body. Determine the intensity of the emotion and ask yourself if you have ever felt it before.

• Get closer to the emotion and stop fearing it.

• By curiously studying the emotion, you will eventually manage to see patterns or draw conclusions as well as elicit solutions.

Create a Journal to Monitor Emotions

Through tracking or writing about your emotions in a journal each day, you can make it into a habit to move them to the conscious which grants one more control over them. The following is an exercise that can help track your emotions:

• Draw one square per day and fill it with symbols that correspond to different habits which are known as a minimalist journaling system.

• Within each square and among other things, monitor how you feel each day upon waking up and during the day as well as just before retiring to bed.

• You can use emoticons to make it simple and clear such as emoticons to capture the emotion as anxious, apathetic, motivated, happy, sad, and peaceful. However, you can still use words or any other denotation that suits you.

• The importance of this exercise is that it enables you to accurately reflect on emotional fluctuations and get valuable data on the following:

• What triggers you, for instance, you might realize that after a few days of lacking self-time, you might feel overwhelmed and can prevent the trigger in the future.

• The exercise can help one determine what their emotional cycles are which relates to self-awareness as an integral component of emotional intelligence. The determined emotional cycles can help you prepare and adjust accordingly when interacting with new people.

• Lastly, this exercise will enable one to determine what motivates them such as waking up at six in the morning could be a great motivator for positive moods and making the individual feel energized. For some people taking a walk can inspire them.

How to Use Self-talk

Self-talk is defined as the way your inner voice makes sense of the world around you, and how you communicate with yourself internally. This concept greatly affects how you interact with the world, and how you talk to yourself internally! If your self-talk is negative, then you could be creating unnecessary anxiety and stress as you perceive the world through a negative lens. Black women with positive self-talk tend to see the world more positively and enthusiastically, which can lead them to be more well-rounded and hopeful people in general.

Identify how you treat yourself. It may sound silly but try and view how you talk about yourself and how many times you say negative things to yourself in the span of a day. Whether you need to write a journal or simply take some time to meditate, it can be astonishing sometimes to realize how often we speak to ourselves negatively.

Replace the negative statements in your self-talk with positive ones. When you are becoming aware of how you treat yourself and the world around you, you can begin to replace the negative statements with different neutral or positive words. This will help you feel more positive or at least more neutral about the experiences you are going through.

Change your definitive statements into questions. Definitive emotional statements are the ones we make every day and may not even realize it. For example, when we say things like, "This is impossible!" or "I am never going to finish this," we are ingraining in ourselves a negative slant to these statements. It only increases our stress and stops you from searching for solutions to solve these problems. You only end up feeling more lost and confused.

Visualizations and Affirmations

Affirmations are statements with a positive tone that work to define your goal and desire and improve the way you view yourself. The technique of using affirmations is to repeat them over and over, so they are embedded into your subconscious and you finally start to believe what you are saying. By believing them, you will follow through on them and accomplish whatever goal you have set for yourself. Whether it's about your habits, your personal or professional behavior or your personality, creating an affirmation can help your mindset so you can conquer a goal. Think of it like this. Working out at the gym is for your physical body, and using affirmations is for your mind!

You want to focus on the stage of your life you are in and what you are going through. You want to replace your *"I can't"* with ***"I can."*** You want to remind your unconscious mind about the positives in your life and feel appreciative about the situation you are in (even if it's a tough one!). Instead of saying things like "I am never going to lose this baby weight," or "I will never understand organic chemistry," create positive affirmations to replace the negative thoughts. Instead, replace those sayings with "I am so thankful for a healthy baby and a smooth pregnancy and labor," and "I am so happy I got into one of the top universities in my state."

Here are some simple steps to create the positive affirmation you may need to get you through the day!

1. Use the words I am in a present tense to emphasize to yourself that you ARE going to be doing something and you will implement this behavior and thought immediately into your life. Not future tense - but today!

2. Be positive. Always use an affirmation to say what you want. Don't focus on things you don't want, but what you hope to gain.

3. Be brief and be specific. You want to be focused on what your goal is and exactly what step you need to achieve it.

4. Include an action word so your brain knows that there is some activity involved that you need to do to make this goal happen.

5. Make sure your affirmations are for yourself, not other people. This is something you are going to work towards for yourself and your betterment, not for anyone else. This ensures that you will feel more motivated about conquering the goal.

Repeat your affirmations to yourself every day, preferably out loud and with energy and enthusiasm! Whether it's taking a minute after you have gotten ready in the morning or saying it before bed at the end of a long day, you want to take some time to remind yourself about these statements. If you have a friend or family member that you are close with, you can have them be the ones to remind you about this affirmation throughout your journey to achieving this goal.

Visualization is a technique where you clearly work to visualize the future reality you want to be living in. The clearer and the more detailed your vision is, the more impact it will have on your subconscious mind. It is a powerful tool that can motivate you for future success in your life. For example, athletes are always told to imagine their future success, that they've won the World Series, or that they have won the Super Bowl in the upcoming season. It's not about confidence per say, but about visualizing your goal coming true, and using that feeling to motivate you to make it happen.

Visualization is tied to neurological activity. When we visualize something, our brain's neurons become excited and tell us to follow through on the visual. It creates a neural pathway that prepares our body in a way following the visual we imagined. Even though we haven't physically experienced that vision yet, our brains make it feel very familiar to us so that our body is primed and ready for it to occur.

Process visualization is about the necessary steps you have to complete to achieve the goal. If you're a runner, instead of jumping ahead to finishing the marathon, you have first to imagine yourself competing and running, and training, and sweating, and working out, all the steps you need to accomplish before you make it to the finish line! You create that mental image of the process so that you are more prepared as you endure it.

Taking care of yourself

Taking care of yourself is the way to happiness and to be able to deal with the hardest emotions. The fact that you are alive shows that you have already taken care of yourself. But beyond survival as an end in itself, what do you do to increase your sense of well-being? How do you cultivate positive emotions without falling into old habits of resisting pain? And finally, is it possible to leave our past behind us?

There are three major components to caring for your body's physical health: eating well, exercising regularly, and getting enough restful sleep. As you work on these areas, be sure to seek out the help of professionals when needed and keep on top of things like medical appointments to ensure your overall physical wellbeing.

Eating

What you put into your body sends important messages about how much you value yourself and prioritize leading a healthy life. This subject can fill a book on its own. Essentially, you'll want to consider your current eating habits and strive to make changes to eat right consciously. This includes eating balanced, regularly scheduled meals, including foods that are healthy and nutritious, eating in moderation, listening to your body signals and hunger cues regarding when you are hungry or full, and avoiding pitfalls like emotional eating or fad diets that set the stage for failure. If you struggle with eating issues, seek out the help of your health care provider or better yet, a qualified nutritionist, who can help you find balance in this area.

Exercising

Look at your relationship with exercise and think about what physical activities you currently do and for what reasons. Exercise also plays a role in our level of self-esteem. Did you know that exercise releases hormones that create the same neurological effects as antidepressant medication? Exercise can be highly effective in decreasing depressive moods that can aggravate low self-esteem. I can't emphasize this enough: Make some form of physical activity a regular part of your life. Standing is better than sitting; five minutes spent moving is better than nothing—the point is, every bit helps. Seek out activities and routines that allow you to stay consistent and find enjoyment, with enough variety to stay interested.

One of the best known and most widely adopted stress-reducing exercise disciplines is yoga, which has been practiced for thousands of years. Yoga teachings originated in India and spread initially to China and the rest of Asia, but now yoga studios and classes may be found worldwide. Online courses and demonstrations are available, especially for beginners and intermediates. There are many online demonstrations that help teach you the movements described here, and many other movements as well.

The advantage of attending yoga classes is the role of the instructor, who is trained to guide each movement, making sure it's done correctly, and helping smooth the transition from each position, or asana, to the next. An alternative to yoga is Pilates, which adds special equipment to enhance or extend the movements.

The following stretching exercises include instructions to manage breathing, which contributes to the physical and emotional benefits.

To get you started, the following stretches are inspired by yoga, but do not require attending a yoga class. No special equipment is required, but if you are not going to be stretching on a carpeted floor, consider purchasing a yoga mat to protect your back, knees, and elbows:

The Mountain Pose. Start by standing erect, feet about 12 inches apart, arms at sides, head held up and facing forward. Slowly force your head upwards, towards the ceiling, and push your arms downwards, towards the floor. Be conscious of your feet being flat on the floor, not emphasizing any front, back or side movement. Tighten your thighs and rear and pull up your kneecaps. Breathe in and out deeply and slowly, following the instructions on managed breathing in the next section. Try to concentrate on what you feel, keeping other thoughts from intruding. Hold this position for two minutes, then relax. If you've held this position and managed your breathing effectively, you will feel the tension slowly starting to subside.

Rising Cobra. Next, stand at the end of the mat and drop to your knees, then extend fully out so you are on your stomach, chin touching the mat, and hands next to shoulders, palms facing downward. To be clear, your body should be fully extended, head to toe flat and downward. Okay? Now, use your hands to push your head and upper body slowly upward, an inch or two at a time. Keep your head steady, facing forward as you rise upward until you feel your lower back letting you know it's time to stop. Hold the position, inhaling and exhaling fully and slowly, for ten seconds, then slowly lower back down to the ground. Relax, take two or three breaths, then repeat the stretch four more times. At the end, stay flat, take a few breaths, and relax. Maintain your position for the next stretch

Cat and Cow. For this move, simply push your upper body up again as before, then slide back over your knees until your thighs are pointing straight downward and pull your hands back until your arms are straight and below your shoulders. In other words, you should now be on your hands and knees, back parallel to the floor. Your hands are below your shoulders and your hips are above your knees. Your head may face forward or downward, whichever is more comfortable. Now, arch your back like an angry cat, stretching upwards towards the ceiling. Breathe in deeply, extending your diaphragm. Hold for a few seconds, then slowly begin to exhale and pull in the diaphragm. As you do so, lower your back as far as you can without straining, pushing your gut towards the floor, so you look like a swayback horse, or a cow. Hold for a few seconds, then head back up again into the angry cat position. Repeat these up and down steps four or more times, then relax.

Bowing Stretch. Ease into the next stretch by moving your upper body back by sliding your rear end backwards, and then press your body down on your calves and heels. Your arms should now be fully extended forward. Keep low so that your chest is now resting on your thighs. If you've done this correctly, your hands and fingers are far forward and your arms are flat on the mat, your face is touching, or almost touching, the mat, and your chest is lying flat on top of your thighs. Your knees will be fully bent, and if they complain (which they may do until you loosen up), raise your rear end a bit to ease the tension, as your knees open up a bit. Take three long, slow inhales and exhales. As with the other stretches, try to extend your diaphragm as you inhale and pull it back in on the exhales. Now, you are ready for the familiar pose known as downward facing dog.

Downward Facing Dog. You've probably seen this stretch in yoga posters or ads because it's popular and it's easy. From the previous bowing stretch, raise your rear end upwards as you push up with your hands. Initially, you will be on your toes, heels raised, and your knees will be bent. Slowly try to straighten your legs and lower your heels. Keep pushing up with your arms and try to straighten them fully. The position you are moving towards culminates with fully extended arms and legs, heels on, or close to, the ground. Keep sliding your hands closer to your feet, if you can, as this will extend the stretch. You should feel the stretch in your back, hamstrings, at the back of your thighs, and in your calves. As with the other stretches, be aware of your breathing and consciously extend and contract your diaphragm.

Tranquility Pose. Now sit down on the floor or mat, then roll over and lay back so you are flat on your back, arms at your sides. Start to roll your legs backwards by raising your knees first, and then lift your feet off the ground and extend your legs upwards towards the ceiling. Your legs may be bent at the knees, so try to extend your feet upward to straighten your legs. Hold this position, take one or two breaths, then continue rolling back so your feet are now over your head. You will feel the stretch in your lower back, which is correct, but don't force it. Slowly lower your feet over your head and continue to try to lower your toes towards the floor behind your head. If you are flexible, you may be able to touch the floor, but if not, just stretch back as far as you can without straining. Be conscious of your breathing and hold this stretch for 20 to 30 seconds, then slowly lower your legs forward to the starting position, flat on your back. Take a few deep breaths. Incidentally, this pose, called tranquility in yoga, is known as the plow, if you are able to reach the floor behind your head with your toes.

Abdominal Tightener. The final stretch continues with you still on your back. Point your toes forward while you extend your arms over your ears and straight back. Pull, to feel your shoulders, toes, and feet extending. Now, press your hands together firmly for up to 10 seconds, then relax. Repeat this, pressing together several times, and as you do so, you should feel a tightening in your abdominal region. This stretch will tighten those "abs," without the potential back strains of traditional sit-ups or crunches.

Stay relaxed, stay positive. When you are finished with your last stretch, it's okay just to lay flat and do nothing. Keep your eyes closed or stare at a spot on the ceiling. Breath slowly and deliberately. Long, slow inhales and long, slow exhales. By being conscious of the breathing, you'll find it easier to keep the odd and unnecessary thoughts from sneaking in. Stay relaxed, feel a sense of inner peace and start to imagine you have a high sense of self-esteem. You are confident, you are optimistic, you are a positive thinker.

Sleeping

Your body does important work while you sleep—this is when it restores and repairs itself! To feel at your best, ensure you are consistently getting enough restful sleep. Poor sleep can leave you feeling irritable and thus more vulnerable to the anxious and negative self-talk messages that chip away at self-esteem. If sleep is an issue for you, it can be helpful to create a structured routine around bedtime. Turn off electronics an hour or two before bed, drink some chamomile tea, and spray a little lavender on your pillow. Instead of falling asleep to the television, offer yourself gentler options like a light read or a meditation.

Soften our body

How do you take care of yourself physically? How do you relate to your body when it is under stress? A compassionate response includes physical softening. Compassion is sweetness and tenderness. However, when we go through difficult times, the sweetness goes away.

Our muscles protect us from potential dangers by creating a shield against the outside world. Unfortunately, our brains cannot easily distinguish between an external and internal threat, so even when we're worried about an exam, our muscles stiffen. Over time, muscle tension can put an unnecessary amount of stress on all body systems.

If you feel tense while meditating or just sitting, try letting go, relaxing your tummy. It is good to remember that we are not saying "try to relax," which would just put pressure on us trying to feel something you don't really feel. Simply sweeten.

Do the same with the breath. When you are tense your breathing will become short and weak. Try to soften it a little, maybe you can do it by expanding your belly when you inhale and exhale very slowly.

For every time you inhale, exhale twice. Don't worry if your breathing becomes shallow again when you're done.

Anything you do to give relief or comfort to the body when you are under stress falls under the category of physical self-compassion. You might need to get some sleep, eat something, get some exercise or a hot bath, have sex, enjoy solitude, or take a vacation? Give yourself a few minutes to imagine what you might need to let go.

Taking care of yourself physically could also clear your mind. Often the relationship between mind and body is inversely proportional: the mind is activated when the body is inactive and calms down when the body begins to move.

By recognizing how we take care of ourselves, we can increase our strengths and remind ourselves of our good habits when under pressure.

Please think of kindness in terms of genuine care as something that makes you feel really good. For example, you might enjoy a cup of hot chocolate in the morning much more than coffee, even though adults drink coffee. Listen to yourself because you know exactly what comforts you and gives you relief. Pay special attention to what you need when you are under severe stress or when things are really bad.

Be friendly with your feelings

How do you take care of your emotional state? The compassionate way to be friends with painful emotions is to stop fighting them. There are many words to describe this attitude: empathy, concern, kindness, care, forgiveness, pity, kindness, tolerance, acceptance, understanding, support ...

Forgiveness is a very important aspect of emotional healing, however many of us find it extremely difficult to forgive ourselves after a mistake. We can't get compassion to reach us.

However, engaging in enjoyable activities can help us, such as:

· Listen to music

· Go on vacation

· Fly a kite

· Think about sex

· Go to church

· Read a novel

· Garden

· Go to the cinema

· Cook something good

Keeping yourself engaged in inherently pleasurable activities, rather than what we perceive as a duty, is a great way to take care of our emotional self.

Relate to others

Entering into a relationship with others is another way to take care of ourselves, let's stop isolating ourselves! Remember that feeling of connection with the sharing of humanity as part of the definition of self-compassion.

A sense of isolation could even turn a completely common sense of unhappiness into despair or a mild anxiety into fear or dread. We may not even notice when our social support network dwindles, as isolation is an error of omission, it is a problem we cannot actually see. Precisely for this reason we should pay particular attention to our relational world.

Kindness in relationship means having our actions guided by the desire to help others and refraining from harming them. The Dalai Lama calls this "wise selfishness" since it encourages others to be kind to us. Furthermore, the memory of a "hot" interaction can give us continuous happiness.

Our behavior impacts others, whether positive or negative, in many different ways and trying to help others can become a habit and bring peace and happiness into our lives.

Practicing Your Appreciation

It has been shown that when you practice appreciation there seems to be a lot of positive outcomes that come of it for the person that shows it and for the person who receives it. Many people have benefited from this since it has long-lasting effects on people. This is why it is worth having just a little bit of it as you go on with your day.

If it was for a small thing or a more significant thing, the point that matters is that you tell them whether it's to their face or not. When you tell someone that they are appreciated for the things they do, can bring a very positive effect just by how the negativity is seen.

Investigating Care

As soon as you find out that something is wrong and you find yourself getting upset as the best option, then you should now that being caring can help a lot with changing the way you feel.

Pursue the TEARS of HOPE direction and set aside the effort to comprehend why you might react along these lines. Care can enable you to discover the headspace to do this in a positive manner.

Reacting Instead of Responding

When we know the difference between reacting and responding it can be a good thing to have. It is also important because of the way our emotions can cause us to react fast. When we become furious, sometimes we are unable to control it and end up screaming at others. For times that we feel pity towards others, we might see ourselves not getting involved with them.

Here and there we have to follow up on these motivations, however, for the most part, we don't. By investigating your negative emotions you can begin to build up your comprehension of how you respond, and rather begin to change this to positive methods for reacting – which could mean discovering that no response is required by any means.

Know when a break is needed

Make sure to know when to take a break. This is important especially when you see yourself surrounded by negativity throughout the day. Listen to your body because it will know when to tell you that you need a break.

If you can, take more than one break. Make sure that you surround yourself with only positivity and do things that you love to do. This will help re-energize you and will allow you to be more productive in your day today.

No matter how you feel, it only matters how you are as a normal person. You may see only a few of these being effective or maybe none. Make sure that you check out a few of them for yourself before you choose one.

Surround Yourself with Positive Energy

A positive frame of mind will shape our perceptions of the world around us. Negative self-talk is often accompanied by increased feelings of stress and feeling like your current situation is "impossible." It will make your inner voice a pessimist and your entire thought process will become negative whenever you encounter a new challenge or opportunity. This severely limits your experiences in the world, and color the way you react to what is happening to you. It can lead to mental health problems and feelings of inadequacy and insecurity.

To maintain a more positive frame of mind and cultivate a positive mode of self-talk, it's important that you immerse yourself in positivity. Whether it's what you're doing or whom you're spending time with, a shift in positivity could improve your feelings of self in the long run.

Surround yourself with positive people. Have you heard the saying "You are the company you keep"? It's true that good traits rub off on people. If you are spending your time with uplifting, energetic, and positive-minded friends and family, you will begin to soak in that environment and feel happier. These friendships should provide you support, encouragement, and comfort when you are down. Pay attention to the people in your life, especially if you feel caught in unnecessary emotional drama or stress. Sometimes, the best course for righting your self-esteem is to cut those relationships from your life and form new, healthy bonds that will nurture and cultivate your positive energy.

Listen to uplifting music. Music is a powerful mood lifter and studies show that it can even ease pain and anxiety in patients. Neurological scans of the brain prove that our cells are activated by music. To surround yourself with positive energy, try picking familiar music that you have memories associated with, like your first concert or first CD you bought. Pick pieces that you feel connected to and react to in a good way. Instead of constantly having your brain run over all the activities of the days, problems at work, your mother's nagging, or student loan debts, fill your environment with songs that make you feel better and offer you an escape from your daily life. Don't forget that classical music can also set a very relaxing mood. Instrumental music is also a great alternative to have in the background as you go about your chores and get ready for bed.

Fill your free time with activities. If you find chunks of free time in your day where you are doing nothing but stressing, fill that time with more productive activities. Whether it's working out, taking an art class or volunteering, it can be any activity you feel passionate about and where your interests lie. Fill your schedule with positive activities that invite new experiences and new people into your life.

Create a gratitude journal. This is an effective strategy often prescribed by mental health professionals. It is a great way to take some time every day and jot down what you are thankful for and what is going right in your life.

POSITIVE AFFIRMATIONS
FOR BLACK WOMEN

An inspirational self-care guide including powerful
affirmations, tips, and specific meditation practices to
help black women find emotional balance and
rediscover their own identity

Dolores Maikee

INTRODUCTION

There's something to be said about punching yourself (and your friends) on the back. Positive affirmations are words that can help you improve your attitude on life if you repeat them to yourself or write them down in a notebook on a regular basis. While affirmations are not a replacement for professional aid such as counselling for dealing with anxiety or depression, individuals who swear by the power of positive language report that it boosts their self-esteem and improves their thinking. If you want to improve your mental health, this is a terrific — and free — place to start.

Furthermore, it may assist improve your general health. According to research, the words we use matter: a good positive affirmation can help you overcome stress and build neuronal connections in your brain. Other studies has showed that repeating them aloud or writing them down might help pupils feel more at home in school, which can lead to better marks.

Affirmations are statements that claim the presence or truth of something. Positive affirmations are simply statements of positive thoughts that are valuable to you. Yes, affirmations might appear corny on the surface, but this does not have to be the case.

Affirmations can help you overcome sentiments of self-worth and self-love. Even if you only commit to jotting down one to three affirmations every day for a month, odds are you'll notice a significant change in your general outlook and self-esteem. Because, let's face it, the true glow-up isn't exterior. The real transformation occurs when you learn to love and accept yourself just as you are.

Do you want to transform your life and your way of thinking? One method is to use positive statements about ourselves or our life, sometimes known as positive affirmations.

What Are Affirmations, And Do They Work?

Affirmations are positive statements that can assist you in challenging and overcoming self-defeating and negative beliefs. When you say them frequently and believe in them, you might begin to see good results. Affirmations may appear to you to be unrealistic "wishful thinking." But consider positive affirmations in this way: many of us conduct repetitive workouts to improve our physical health, and affirmations are similar to mental and emotional exercises. Positive mental repetitions can rewire our thinking habits, causing us to think – and behave – differently over time.

Evidence shows that affirmations can help you perform better at work, for example. According to studies, spending only a few minutes before a high-pressure meeting – such as a performance review – may soothe your anxiety, boost your confidence, and raise your chances of a favourable outcome.

Self-affirmation can also help to relieve stress. In one research, a quick affirmation exercise boosted the problem-solving ability of "chronically stressed" people to the same level as those with less stress. Affirmations have also been used successfully to assist those suffering from low self-esteem, depression, and other mental health difficulties. They have also been shown to trigger regions of our brains that make us more eager to make healthy changes.

According to a recent study, having a better feeling of self-worth makes you more inclined to enhance your own well-being. If you're concerned that you eat too much and don't get enough exercise, for example, using affirmations to remind yourself of your beliefs might motivate you to improve your behavior.

How To Start Using Positive Affirmations

To begin, pay attention to whether ideas, emotions, or behaviors are working against you. If you need assistance in detecting dangerous practices, our well-being quiz might assist you.

However, be cautious since simply repeating any old positive affirmation will most likely not result in meaningful improvement. If we want our positive affirmations to be effective, we must first understand how to create positive affirmations correctly. Our positive affirmations are more likely to result in more good acts, feelings, and experiences this way. So, keep these pointers in mind while you create positive affirmations.

1. Speak and Repeat Positive Affirmations Out Loud

Speaking helps strengthen our learning and raises the possibility that our subconscious will hear our request. Including additional senses can assist much more. Lighting a candle or a stick of incense each time you say your affirmations, for example, is a means of connecting the positive affirmation to other anchors in your surroundings. Over time, merely the light from the candle or the fragrance of the incense can stimulate the brain areas involved with positive affirmation. By developing a habit like this that is repeated on a regular basis and is related to the affirmations, you are forming brain connections that can strengthen the affirmation.

2. Use the Present Tense When Saying Positive Affirmations

Concepts such as "sooner," "later," or "better" are confusing and might cause your affirmation to lose focus and potency. So keep your optimistic affirmations brief and your statements in the present tense. "I am healthy and happy," for example, rather than "I shall be happy soon." It's more of a comfort than a goal. By being specific and stating in the term that we already are or have what we want, we begin to generate the feelings that result from the statement being true.

3. Avoid negatives in positive affirmations

Avoid using negativity in your affirmations. For example, if your positive affirmation is "I am no longer unwell," your thinking is focused on avoidance (of the negative) rather than approach (of the good). Similarly, stating "I am done with toxic relationships" may backfire since it focuses on poor connections rather than good ones. Instead, concentrate your affirmation on the best-case scenario.

Your positive affirmations should aim to convey your wishes as actual, rather than focused on your dissatisfactions. Choose your message with care to ensure that your words reflect the good present and future you wish to build.

4. Create positive affirmations that are meaningful to you

Some basic affirmations, such as "I am confident" or "I am happy," might feel a little strained, causing some conflict between the words and your present sentiments about yourself. If you're feeling this way, consider coming up with affirmations that seem authentic to you. "I am capable of manifesting my dreams," for example, or "I am someone who can welcome love into my life." Affirmations may be quite personal, and their effectiveness may be determined in part by how these words connect with you as a unique individual.

5. Craft positive affirmations that are specific, simple, and direct

Your conscious mind understands what it wants, but it needs your unconscious mind's permission. So be as explicit as possible. "I make $100,000 a year running my own purpose-driven business," for example. "I feel like I'm making a difference, and I have plenty of time to spend with family and friends." Once you've created a thorough positive affirmation that you like, try it out and see how you feel. If your affirmation does not make you feel better, rewrite it until it does.

6. Fill your positive affirmations with passion

Positive affirmations with emotion and real believe have a bigger impact. Feeling the change you desire to see aids the effectiveness of your positive affirmations. So, try this: "I am happy," you say. Now pause and recall a time when you were truly joyful, and reconnect with that sensation. Try to appreciate the sensation and get the most out of it as possible.

Say "I am happy," and actually radiate what happiness feels like when you do so. Affirmations may be far more successful in bringing about what you want if they are filled with pleasant feelings.

7. Add visualizations to your positive affirmations

Create a situation in your conscious mind that supports your optimistic affirmations. This exercise, or visualization, is an amazing option to communicate your desires to your subconscious mind. For example, if you're looking for a home, imagine the house of your dreams, whether it's a small cottage in the woods or a palace on the hill, and bring it to life in your mind, complete with all the features, sensations, scents, noises, and colors. The more clearly you can visualize what you want to produce, the more powerful your affirmation will be.

8. Ground your positive affirmations in your body

Facial expressions, gung-ho gestures, thumbs-up, affirmative sounds like "Whoah!" or "Yes I can!", clap your hands, or jump up and down are all appropriate. Exercising or going for a stroll while repeating your affirmations is another approach to get your message into your body. As a result, the mental-somatic connections in the brain are strengthened, which might give more support for your positive affirmation.

9. Take action on your positive affirmations

Take some action to put your positive affirmations into action. Send out some resumes if you're seeking for work. If you want to become in shape, repeat your affirmations as you walk or drive to the gym. If you want to establish a business that you enjoy, you should start working on it right away. Words are not as powerful as actions.

10. Stick to your positive affirmations

Reprogramming your brain takes time. Put up sticky note reminders throughout your house, paint a rock as a trigger-reminder, or change your cellphone lock screen to remember yourself to practice your positive affirmations. Declare your positive affirmation aloud whenever you see or think of your thing. You may also mail yourself a letter or set a reminder in your digital calendar to practice positive affirmation. Above everything, be consistent and persistent.

POSITIVE AFFIRMATIONS FOR BLACK WOMEN

Black women are strong and powerful. They are queens and all-powerful creators. This is a huge duty, but it's also a huge burden that can bring grief and anguish at times. This affirmation book is written particularly for black women to help them deal with the pain from their past that is still present in their lives today. It will bring forth hope, peace, love, and happiness. It is for the worst days conceivable in order for them to become the finest days imaginable.

Given that February is Black History Month and that I am a black woman, I was inspired to write a piece about positive affirmations for black women.

I am the Queen of Affirmations; I wholeheartedly believe in them!

I believe in setting goals that you can strive towards, but I also believe that utilizing positive affirmations on a regular basis can help you become more optimistic and feel more in charge of yourself.

The more affirmations I say and believe, the more successful I am.

I'm so delighted you're here today if you believe in affirmations like I do!

As a black woman, I wanted to encourage other women of color to practice regular affirmations.

I'm hoping that these joyful black woman affirmations will help me feel accomplished and strong.

I know I've come to rely on them over the years.

Powerful Affirmations For Black Women:

- We are powerful, beautiful beings, and I know this is difficult for people to believe.
- But when put to the test, I genuinely think we can conquer anything. Sometimes we simply need a little support to get through, but you can do it most of the time.
- Here's how to have faith in yourself - Use and speak these strong black affirmations on a regular basis, preferably in the morning.
- You might also jot down 4-5 of these that truly connect with you on a sticky note and post it to your computer, mirror, fridge, or car so you can read it out loud whenever you want.
- The more you repeat it, the more you believe it and the more you take action to become a better version of yourself.

Inspiring black affirmations for black women:

- I realize the greatness that exists inside me.
- I embrace personal responsibility for my own happiness and growth.

- I'm putting together a network of people that will inspire and motivate me.

- I am proud of my culture, background, and experiences because they shaped who I am. I am a strong black woman who deserves all the wonderful things that come my way. I am choosing not to wait to be picked.

- I breath assurance and expel skepticism.

- The things that set me apart are the things that make me ME – (A. A. Milne) I have the ability to effect change.

- I am better than I was yesterday, and I will not allow society to define who I am.

Self-love affirmations for black women:

- It is important to love oneself.

- First and foremost, you are stunning; everyone is stunning in their own right. This is something I want you to be aware of.

- When you question yourself, repeat these self-love affirmations aloud and believe.

- I have control over how I feel, and today I am choosing happy.

- I'm confident enough that I was formed this way for a reason, so I'm going to put it to use

- I am a blessing magnet; I am at ease in my own flesh; and I am deserving of pleasure and success.

- I am overjoyed, happy, and in love.

- I have a positive self-image.

- I am a stunning ebony woman.

Motivation affirmations for black women:

- I am dedicated to my own achievement.

- I am grateful for the numerous gifts in my life. I know things can become rough out there, but I know I was born to be great – Danai Gurira

- My decisions and actions lead to my achievement.

- I can achieve anything I set my mind to. Attracting more success comes easily and effortlessly to me. I am committed to reaching my objectives.

- I am drawing riches and prosperity into my life because I am devoted to my own success.

- I'm taking action on my goals right now so that I may live the life I want.

Positive affirmations for attracting money for women of color:

- In my life, I would like to have an infinite source of income and fortune.

- In my life, there is always more than enough money.

- My income is always increasing, and every dollar I spend and gift is multiplied. I choose to live a wealthy and fulfilling life.

Finding Emotional Balance.

Thousands of thought-provoking published book/articles about the pandemic, the Black Lives Matter Movement, unemployment, civic unrest, police brutality, and the economy are available. In the meantime, we're still here. Some of us are barely hanging on and are in a state of anguish. I am a black lady in excruciating pain. I'm observing the continued aggression against my community while also knowing that we're dying at a higher rate as a result of this sickness. What can we do to help ourselves heal? Holding room for all of this discussion while also caring for our own mental health may be exhausting. A knowledgeable and compassionate guide to emotional and mental wellness for women of all ages.

Women are twice as likely as males to suffer from depression. While women seek therapy for mental problems at a higher rate than males, they also want to help others, attempting to make everyone happy while caring for parents, husbands, and children. Doing it all might be exhausting at times. Everyone goes through seasons of melancholy, as well as times of anxiety and nervousness. But what if those sensations don't go away? Too frequently, women of color attempt to overcome depression and anxiety on their own. This is especially concerning for minority women. women are at least twice as likely as males to undergo a serious deep depression. In addition, as compared to Caucasian women, African-American women are just half as likely to seek aid.

Make Mental Health Your Priority

The traditional notion that only persons who are "mad" or "weak" see mental health specialists contributes to the difficulty in obtaining assistance. "There's a belief in many black communities that women must be tough and stoic," Richards says. "Women are so preoccupied with taking care of everyone else — their partners, their aging parents, and their children — that they neglect themselves." Women, on the other hand, should be reminded that catering to their own needs, whether physical or emotional, does not imply weakness. It improves your ability to care for your loved ones in the long run." There is no substitute for the assistance of a mental health expert.

However, you can protect your mental health by engaging in the following self-care activities:

- **Get plenty of sleep:** Aim for at least seven hours of sleep every night. Sleep deprivation disrupts your emotions, making everything you do less efficient.

- **Move more:** Exercise for 30 minutes every day to improve your health and release feel-good endorphins, which can help some individuals manage or prevent depressive symptoms.

- **Eat healthily:** A balanced combination of fruits, vegetables, and protein maintains energy levels, allowing you to better handle the ups and downs of your day.

- **Connect:** Make time once a week to catch up with a friend, even if it's only for a cup of coffee or a walk. Several studies have indicated that social support improves women's mental health by lowering stress and the effects of depression.

- **Meditate:** People who participated in an eight-week mindfulness meditation course saw improvements in their despair, anxiety, and pain symptoms.

- **Know your limits:** Avoid demands that cause unneeded stress, such as hosting parties or organising events, as much as feasible. Setting limits at work, such as not checking email after a particular time, can also aid in stress reduction.

How Black Women Can Address Workplace Wellness and Leaders Can Make Workplaces Fair and Inclusive

Here are additional tips:

- Understand the anxiety that comes with feeling invisible. "There is a lack of awareness and empathy, particularly when discussing recent instances, of how news and trauma effect Black women directly."

- Address the issue of lack of assistance. Shifts and adjustments can be made by company executives. "That may be acknowledging that complicated family situations necessitate more employment flexibility."

- Allow for genuine selves. "Black women must project a positive image of themselves and engage in self-monitoring." They can't be themselves when chatting about music or television. "Black ladies must concentrate on their image management."

- Create a sense of community by forming Employee Resource Groups based on demographics. "Create an area where users may find content that is relevant to their interests."

Let Me Tell You Something, Your Mental Health Is Vital

What is going on right now is communal trauma compounded by generational trauma. Every time I see photographs, videos, or images of black people being murdered, it triggers a micro-trauma in me. To live, I must rely on healing-centered practices and coping skills. We all process and deal in our own unique ways. When I say I'm actively engaged in self-care, I don't mean taking a bubble bath. I'm a black woman living in America who is navigating "the system" while dealing with her own past trauma and survivorship (suicide, sexual violence). Self-care is a full-time job for me. For me, it generally begins with a series of questions such as, "Is this going to be beneficial or detrimental to my mental health?"

I am someone who has been "trained" to prioritize what other people believe and need over my own wellbeing. That achievement involves compartmentalization and commitment. (And the award goes to...) I've been advised that taking care of myself is "selfish" and that my productivity is related to my value. These are falsehoods at best, and a tactic to keep me out of my own power and down the impostor syndrome rabbit hole. Some of my continuing work is creating greater healing focused practices of connecting with myself. This includes

162

counseling and meditation (though that has been challenging lately) (though that has been difficult lately).

Here is a list of things to think about when it comes to self-care. They may seem easy, but they needed a significant amount of "de-programming." Recognize that you should do what works for you and trust your instincts. Please take what is useful and discard what isn't:

1. **Reach Out To Trustworthy People Who Can Hold Space For You.**

Even if they genuinely care about you, not everyone can be supportive. Consider the people who will be there, and make it simple to be yourself. There will be no performances or faking it, just being. This is more difficult when you are portrayed as "the strong black woman," and asking for help is perceived as weak. Those are all falsehoods. Isolation and silence can exacerbate discomfort. Connecting with ourselves and others who support us is vital.

2. **Connect With Things That Bring You Joy Or Energy**

It may seem tough or even impossible right now, but if you have the potential... It is something I would suggest. When one of my friends asked how she could help, I told her to email me images of her child playing. I'm creating affirmations about my own identity, potential, and value. I'm listening to music that nourishes my spirit and seeing media that energizes rather than depletes me. I'm watching Insecure and The Photograph (all Issa Rae), but only shows that promote positive and complex black identities. I need our black love stories, supernatural stories, science-fiction stories, and other non-painful depictions of our existence. It reminds me of the entire scene.

3. **Ask Yourself What You Want And Need Right Now, And Then Advocate For It**

- Do you want a break from your work? Can you request time off or a variety of choices? If not, are you able to use your paid time off (PTO)?
- Is it time to look into therapy? Do you require peer support?
- Do you want to engage in-depth, mediated discussions regarding racism and pain? Can you participate in a healing circle?
- Do you have to stop talking about racism and pain in order to check out?
- Do you want your friends and coworkers to send you check-in text messages and phone calls?
- Do you need to ignore text messages and phone calls for a bit and become silent?
- Understand what you require from the people around you and be sure to share it.

4. **Revisit Your Coping Mechanisms And Remove Those That No Longer Serve You**

I'm not here to pass judgment on your coping strategies; you needed them to live, and they helped you at some time in your life. However, it may be time to reconsider if they are still useful.

My previous coping mechanisms included:

- I was so preoccupied with work projects or activism that I avoided confronting my own thoughts and emotions.

- People-pleaser

- I avoided any "conflict" or stating what I truly felt since I knew the consequence would be ineffective. People can surprise you occasionally, and sometimes they don't, but I won't know if I don't use my voice. (*Please keep in mind that it is still vital for me to speak what I believe and feel in order to be honest to myself. I understand that not everyone has such privilege or safety.)

- I devoted all of my care and energy to "helping others," which left me emotionally famished (but feeling good because I could avoid paying attention to my own life)

- Insert if you're numbing out emotions with food or binge-watching Netflix. (there are many more)

5. Allow Yourself To Feel Your Emotions And Attend Your Physical Needs

Whether I'm feeling pain or anger, I'm allowing myself to sit in those unpleasant areas and release those sensations rather than shoving them down. This also entails paying close attention to your body. Do you feel an urge to go for a walk? Do you get enough sleep? Are you thirsty? Is there physical pain in your body that has to be released? I'm still a work in progress, but I've observed that if I don't make time and space for releasing, it pours out in unhelpful ways.

6. **Transform Feelings Of Hopelessness To Advocacy**

Turning my sadness into action benefits my mental health and allows me to channel that negative energy into something constructive. Feeling your emotions is beneficial, and checking out may be essential. Both have their own time and place. This list is highly recommended for those of you seeking for methods to assist through contributions or education. I take breaks and love unplugging with a good plan or a book, but I try not to use it to detach from myself.

7. **Create Boundaries For Yourself Of What Works Specifically For YOU**

No. = A complete sentence.

Telling someone no used to cause panic, dread, and condemnation. (It was particularly difficult for me because I used to associate my value with productivity and people-pleasing.) Boundaries enable me to maintain honest, balanced, and healthy relationships. Here are some of the questions I ask myself to help me recognize my limits.

- Is this something I'm doing because I'm compelled, guilty, or under pressure?
- Is it necessary for me to have this talk right now?
- Is this exhausting or energetic?
- Is it necessary for me to take a vacation from social media, the news cycle, and certain conversations?
- Is it necessary for me to _____(insert items) right now? Ever?

8. Is it mine to do?

Don't forget to take breaks, breathe deeply, drink plenty of water, and explore with your wants. Consider engaging with great black art, culture, and music that tell a different story about our lives and our strength. Please add to this list and discuss what works for you. We require your assistance.

SELF-LOVE FOR BLACK WOMEN

Black people are naturally gorgeous and strong. As a result, Black people must treat themselves with respect. Most Black people grow up learning to cope rather than learning to heal and care for themselves. Too frequently, learning to adapt entails learning survival tactics that foster problematic codependency on external sources. The truth is that all of the care that Black people require is found inside themselves.

Healing and self-care are all about finding inner peace in the midst of a chaotic environment. Self-care should never be a one-time event. Discipline and consistency are essential for self-care. You must reach a point where you love yourself so much that you decide to make yourself your top priority every day; you must allow this to become normal. When you practice self-care, you get clarity, a greater sense of purpose, and the ability to show up healthier in your personal relationships.

Racism isn't going away tomorrow, but it doesn't mean Black people should suffer in silence. Black people must actively explore ways to increase self-love and harmony in themselves and the Black community as a whole. People of color should not see themselves as always buried in white supremacy. An inferiority complex is the belief that you have little control over your life. Black people must understand that self-love and emancipation originate from inside, and that you can choose to take care of yourself at any time.

Wellness enables you to heal through holistic methods. Holistic techniques allow you to trust yourself and allow the environment to flood back into your body and mind. Believe it or not, self-care is not consumerism, it is not materialism, it does not have a look, it is not classicist, and it does not have a body type. There is no such thing as self-care. Self-care has no age limit. Self-Care is not mutually exclusive. Every human being on this earth needs to practice self-care. Black people are smart individuals who must begin to care for themselves not just on the surface but also on the inside.

Here are 25 self-care tips that will help you to achieve inner peace and healing:

1. Disconnect from social media

Low self-esteem and sleep deprivation have been directly connected to social media activity. Constant exposure to videos and photos of Black people being killed and attacked may also have an impact. Unplugging from social media helps you to detox from a confined environment, reconnect with the present moment, and improve attention. Bonus: You may erase your applications for several hours or days at a period, and you'll be surprised at how much you can get done when you're not connected.

169

2. Develop a healthy relationship with food

Allow yourself to eat food that feeds and energizes you rather than food that depletes your body's energy reserves.

3. Celibacy

We live in an era where the Black body is oversexualized. Abstinence and celibacy, on the other hand, may be extremely uplifting and healing. Celibacy forces your body to seek pleasure in ways other than sex, resulting in a deeper sense of self. You can experiment with it for a week, a month, or as long as you like.

4. Eliminate stressful situations

Society has taught us that high levels of stress and life are inextricably linked, yet this is a lie. Stress is a normal part of our lives, but it should never feel draining or depleting. Begin by identifying the sources of your everyday stress and setting objectives to remove or address what is draining your energy. Don't be frightened to move ahead if something has taken a toll on you. By removing difficult events from our life, we make room for greater things to arrive.

5. Buy Black-owned

There is no higher feeling than knowing you have made a contribution to the Black economic structure. Supporting Black-owned means you are supporting black people's economic independence. Whenever you are in the market for something, look for a black-owned business before buying outside of black and brown areas.

6. Attend a local yoga and meditation class — or do it at home daily

Previously, it was assumed that the brain develops with age. Meditation, on the other hand, has been shown to improve one's sense of well-being. Meditation alters the expression of our DNA in our cells, allowing us to respond to stress in a more peaceful manner. There are many of yoga and meditation applications available to help you get started.

7. Zen your home

Ambiance is important for relaxation and self-care. Light some candles, burn some sage, and saturate your house with aromatherapy and the delectable aromas of essential oils. Just breathe while listening to jazz. Calming your own surroundings will provide you with a tremendous sense of serenity.

8. For vs against

Make the choice to stand up for something you believe in rather than battling against something you dont. Pursue activism without encountering difficulty. Activism does not imply a lack of peace; in contrary, activists require a great deal of peace. As activists, black people must approach issues with reasoning rather than passion. When you are battling something that is proof that you need to remove yourself out of the battlefield, you must take time to love yourself and not be so tied to the results you are attempting to promote that you neglect your own recovery.

9. Reconnect with family

Making contact with family relatives may be an exciting form of generational love and unconditional support. This is not to say that there should be no limits or family members with whom you have severed contact. Find a family member to call on a weekly or monthly basis. Black families have an uncanny capacity to provide love and support that no one else can.

10. Make a "you" day

Make one day a week, or a few days a week, your personal day. Set aside one day every week for "you." There will be no job or responsibilities, simply a day to spend with yourself doing whatever you want. That time may be spent cleaning, reading, watching a movie, going out to dinner with friends, or doing anything you like. Just make sure you're the first one there that day to provide the groundwork for this mindset to become a daily habit.

11. Attend a retreat

Retreats provide an opportunity to get away from enormous crowds, drinking, and the everyday "turn-up" mentality. Retreats are designed to help you calm down, contemplate, and fall in love with yourself. Furthermore, retreats include guilt-free meals, healthy lifestyle adjustments, and encouragement to bring happiness into your life.

12. Volunteer or donate

Serving others not only brings personal joy, but it also benefits everyone! Healing occurs when we recognize that we all have a purpose and that we are all part of the solution. Sign a petition or donate and volunteer your time at Black-owned businesses to save mankind.

13. Release an old habit that does not affirm your humanity

It is always a good moment to think on oneself and identify tendencies that may be perpetuating an internalized systemic dehumanization.

14. Become a plant parent, or bask in nature

Go outdoors! Nature is your buddy, and everything in nature exists to help you grow. Endorphins are released while we are in nature, according to science. If you are unable to spend time in nature, adopting and caring for a plant might be soothing.

15. Take personal responsibility

It is extremely healing to accept personal responsibility for the roles you play in your life. Once you understand your job and recognize your shortcomings, you can begin to actually work on yourself. When you are your best self, the world is a better place!

16. Read more books

Reading can send you to a variety of worlds and realms. Reading might also inspire you to come up with fresh ideas. Nothing beats snuggling up and getting lost in a good book. Visit a bookshop and stock up on self-help and empowerment literature.

17. Identify negative-self talk

Recognize when negative self-talk begins and put a stop to it. Choose to express something wonderful about yourself right then and there.

18. Create!

To create is to give birth to all the things you desire to see happen. Allow your imagination to go wild and devote your efforts to a work that offers you a sense of purpose. Make art, make a video, or try your hand at writing. Writing helps you to express yourself freely and without censure. Write something for you!

19. Say yes to more positivity in your life

Accept the possibility of transformation and change. Recognize that everything that happens in your life is ultimately for your own growth and advancement. Align yourself with the cosmos and recognize that everything is occurring for you, not against you. Our consciousness transforms when we realize that things are continually happening for us. We start to see our manifestations flourish, and we can appreciate the beauty of life.

20. Exercise

There are thousands of workout classes available, ranging from Muay Thai to Functional Training to Jogging. Find a class that is a good fit for you and stick with it. Make a commitment to yourself to attend a class for a set period of time until it becomes a habit. Exercise boosts self-esteem, improves stamina during sex, and is generally enjoyable and healthy.

21. Make time for solitude

Spending time alone allows you to properly understand how you feel. Make time for yourself, whether you're in a relationship or a parent. Introverts are misunderstood because seclusion allows you to refocus. It enables you to find answers to your inquiries without being interrupted. Being alone is like being in a moving meditation.

22. Travel

Buy a flight ticket to a location you've only visited in your fantasies. Go trekking and try cuisine from all around the world. Meet the people and become immersed in the culture. Traveling bestows gratitude and a global connection on the traveler.

23. Use crystal healing

Crystals have energy vibrations that can cure, according to science. Try black tourmaline to balance negative and good energy, rose quartz to attract more love into your life, and caracole to soothe a stressed, workaholic soul. You can deal with thousands of different crystals.

24. Give yourself a makeover

When you change your look, you may feel a rebirth. Get a fresh hairstyle or try on a different outfit. You'll be surprised at how much confidence you'll get as a result.

25. Realize Your Worth

Know that you are always worthy of dignity and respect. Your worth or value is not determined by your job, education, or status. Your value is your natural right. You are deserving of dignity and respect simply because you are a living human being. Love yourself and constantly remember that you are priceless.

WHY SELF-LOVE AND SELF-CARE ARE RADICAL FOR BLACK WOMEN

Historically, people that fall under the most susceptible intersections of identities have been the most significantly impacted during times of instability. As a Black queer immigrant woman travelling across the globe, the upheaval of our political, social, and environmental disorder has compounded the daily oppressions that I encounter from racism, sexism, homophobia, and xenophobia. More often than not, black women are the primary caregivers for their families, households, and communities. This is reinforced not only by a plethora of facts, but also by a long history based in slavery. Who cares about us when our livelihoods are jeopardized by inflexible institutional forces that prioritize profit above people?

According to the National Study of Women's Health, "black women are 7.5 years physiologically 'older' than white women... Our telomeres (chromosome ends that govern aging and other critical biological activities) are physically decreasing as a result of oxidative stress causes such as daily racism." Combine that with increased black maternal mortality rates, particularly among academics, and the unfair pay gap for Black women, who get 61 cents for every dollar earned by their white, male counterparts, and we have some grim statistics. It is now more important than ever for Black women and women of color to prioritize their mental, emotional, and physical health. Self-care has devolved into a murky, commodified phrase that corporate marketers (particularly those in the beauty sector) use to boost revenue. But, other from face masks and crystals, what does a radical, substantive, self-care framework for Black women look like outside of capitalism?

Grounding our self-care in radical self-love

We live in a culture and era that profit off Black bodies and identities' self-hatred. As self-care activist Sonya Renee Taylor points out, our fights against oppressive societal constructions ultimately begin with "our political, social, and interpersonal ties with other people's bodies." And it begins with us as people, with our interactions with our own bodies." As Black women, the personal and political are inextricably linked. We may destroy the master's tools and destabilize power structures that rely on our self-deprecation by anchoring our action in our own radical, unconditional love.

We all share the experience of having a body, and our bodies are responsible for many of the events that occur in the world. As a result, it stands to reason that our road to successful self-care should begin with unconditional love for our bodies. Grounding my self-care in appreciation for my body and making thankfulness a continuous habit in my life has drastically changed the way I move through my life.

Prioritizing our holistic health

An old adage says that you can't pour from an empty cup, yet this is easier said than done. I frequently find myself pushing myself to see how effective I can be at work, in my relationships, and in my personal pursuits. Even when my body shows indications of weariness or dehydration, my inner critic is never pleased and constantly pushes me to do more.

On a particularly exhausting day, as I struggled for a seat on the packed New York subway, it came to me: If I don't put myself first, who will? This simple yet revolutionary question grounds me anytime I feel bad for having a sick day or blame myself for not finishing that assignment. Prioritizing my emotional, mental, and spiritual wellness is neither selfish nor indulgent; it is, nevertheless, ultimately vital for me to present my best self.

How do you maintain self-love? Practice!

It's difficult to overlook the signs urging you to take time out for yourself if you've made it a part of your regular routine. If you make daily affirmations a part of your routine, for example, you'll find yourself saying them every time you look in the mirror. It only takes a few days to become a habit, and self-love may quickly become one of your better behaviors if you make it a routine.

Ways To Practice Self-Love

We are better capable of sharing love with others when we have a solid, unwavering love for ourselves. Here are some strategies for practicing self-love when you need it the most. I am a firm belief that if more individuals had a greater feeling of self-love, the world we live in would be a better, more peaceful place. When you are completely at peace with yourself, the need to compare, attack, and criticize others is almost non-existent, and your capacity to accept the diversity of others soars. You are a calmer, happier person when you are completely at peace with yourself.

The problem is that practicing self-love is difficult. When we have high expectations of ourselves or when the responsibilities of life become too much to handle, our self-esteem is typically the first thing to suffer. Many individuals celebrate the love of a romantic partner or a friend at this time of year. But this year, I want you to focus on celebrating your self-esteem.

Remain Present.

We live in a world that is full with distractions. We have an infinite quantity of information at our fingertips because to cell phones, but we don't have the time or brain ability to process it all. I won't urge you to give up your phone because that's ridiculous, and let's be honest, I'm just as addicted to mine as the next millennial. Instead, choose one thing that you truly enjoy and make it a point to be completely present while doing it. Create a distraction-free zone around the one thing that fills you up the most, whether it's creating, coloring, writing, or enjoying a meal with your loved partner.

Open Yourself Up To Learning.

Nothing beats the thrill of discovering something new. Whether it's taking a class in a subject you'd want to learn more about, acquiring a creative talent like photography or playing a musical instrument, or just asking for clarification when you don't understand something, constant learning is a fantastic confidence booster.

Say No.

This one is especially difficult for women since we are so prone to take care of everyone else before we take care of ourselves. But here's the thing: every time you put someone else's goals ahead of your own, you're saying no to yourself. Know that it is perfectly OK to say no to others in order to say yes to yourself. Instead of quickly saying yes to every request that comes your way, ask for time to think it over so you don't leave yourself running on empty. There is nothing wrong with requesting time to consider things through before taking on tasks for others.

Move Your Body.

Oh, you knew it was coming. Your body is eager to move. On a daily basis This does not imply that you must engage in strenuous exercise every day. That implies you'll need to get up and walk about during the day. Your lovely figure was not made to sit in a chair in front of a computer all day. Leaving aside the issues of weight and appearance, activity is essential if you want to live your happiest, healthiest life. Even a little walk around the block or stretching for a few minutes is a lovely way to practice self-love and appreciation.

Eat More Whole Foods.

It is important to consider how you feed your body. When you consume largely complex carbs, protein, and healthy fats (with plenty of room for sweets, we don't do deprivation here), your body flourishes and you have the energy you need to get through your busy day. Depriving oneself of meals or depending on junk places extra strain on your body, causing it to work harder than required to get through the day.

Take In Positive Words.

Overcoming negative self-talk is difficult, and to be honest, I don't know how to entirely eliminate it. Rather of attempting to silence unpleasant ideas, try to surround yourself with as many positive phrases as possible. Is the music you're listening to full of upbeat, motivating lyrics? Do you have positive affirmations written in a visible place in your home? Instead of just inquiring how your partner's day went, ask, "What was the highlight of your day today?"

Surrounding yourself with good words, even if they aren't your own, may make a big impact in how you start talking to yourself.

Strut Your Stuff.

Even if you're not a fan of being put-together all the time, taking a few additional minutes to feel more put-together may make a big impact. Do the small things that make you feel wonderful, whether it's putting a little more attention into your dress, arranging your hair your favorite manner, or filling in your brows to perfection.

Share Your Gifts.

You have a variety of gifts that the rest of the world has yet to see. Let them out and share them! Even if it's only an idea, discuss it with someone you trust in a private setting. Believing in and sharing your strengths, ideas, and talents is a great act of self-love that may also benefit people around you.

Know Your Worth – And Stick To It.

Okay, folks, this is where things start to get serious. When was the last time you checked in with yourself and assessed your self-worth? We must audit ourselves on a regular basis to ensure that we are actually living in accordance with our principles. Knowing your worth and refusing to allow other pressures compromise your principles is difficult, but it is also extremely gratifying and a brave act of self-love.

Recognize And Embrace Your Weirdness.

You're lying to yourself if you think you're not strange. Everyone is a little odd, and that's what makes life so interesting. I'm sure there are individuals out there that are just as crazy as you and would love and appreciate it if you let your craziness shine. Do s, and don't be scared to embrace your own eccentric oddity.

The Essence Of Meditation For Black Women

For the longest time, little to no attention was paid to the importance of finding a peaceful time and space to listen to the mind and body. It's a busy world filled with busy people trying to juggle their daily activities. It is necessary to work. There have to be enough material resources to help sort out the basic needs and wants. But, there's a need to also capitalize on resources for mental needs. Your body works tirelessly, so that big break to sit and relax can help you become self-aware of your current state of mind. While many people would prefer to relax with a favorite television show, others would prefer to dig into the library for a book. Then, there are the ones that enjoy the mindful art of meditation. This is not a new practice; it's a form of exercise. Exercise that requires that the body does nothing. It is an exercise targeted at helping the mind get rid of all toxicity, be it stress or anxiety. This practice has been going on for centuries. It was traditionally employed to understand and key into the spiritual realm or forces. These days, everyone chooses to indulge in it to gain the natural benefits for better health. The easy-peasy part of it all is that it requires no use of special and expensive equipment. It is simple and can be done anywhere if properly understood.

Black Women And Meditation

Black women have opted to start practicing meditation to find a balance between their bodies' physical and mental state. Many black women are choosing meditation because they have discovered the therapeutic benefits of enjoying a peaceful state. Although it can be quite hard to focus on background noises in the neighborhood, a deep understanding and learning can gradually help sway you off from these distractions easily. Black women go through many things emotionally, physically, and mentally that cause stress. These things can spring up from their places of work, at home, social gatherings, or even within themselves. A little bit of being able to take down these heavy burdens, even if it's for a few minutes, would go a long way. The aim has been to help channel this attention paid to the stress to something else. Then get rid of whatever thoughts pop up in your mind to cause this stress. A director of the University of California at the center for Studying Adversity and Cardiovascular disease, Michelle Albert, M.D, M.P.H, had research carried out. This research indicated that black women record a higher stress level than other races. This makes them more liable to diseases like hypertension, diabetes, obesity, etc. Black women are constantly under certain pressure that increases the rate at which they get stressed. Some of these issues they battle include:

Self Eteem

This is constantly on the increase—the battle of being better, looking better, and feeling better to be validated by society. Black women are unique, beautiful, powerful, and strong. Their accolades from having these natural qualities make them second guess due to certain past issues like racist or sexist discrimination. It is more of a mental than a physical challenge to black women. These conflicting thoughts about their performance can add up to the stress they get to feel every day as they go out and come in.

Negative Thoughts

The human instinct instills fear when we try out new activities. Even actions as basic as living our daily lives can make us fearful. The fear and worries of navigating life's problems can cause unnecessary pressure. This makes it even more difficult to find solutions to the problems. Nobody should live life this way. However, it is not so easy to live without having thoughts about potential disasters and problems. An average black may see this as a measure of preparing themself to face future disappointments. As a result, they condition their minds to worry about things they have no control over, which is not good for mental and physical well-being.

Boredom and Loneliness

In the world we live in today, everyone grows up from being this interactive social being to becoming a busy person. Nobody has time for the other, even when they can certainly create the time to catch up. The average black woman lives on the dream of chasing a career and building a family that can keep the home interesting. When it doesn't work that way, she is faced with the problem of being bored and lonely. Life won't always go on the path we choose for it. Some people may graduate early, get married and build a home. For others, they may need to wait a while longer. Building a home is necessary, but it doesn't have to come with pressure. These things have to flow without being pushed; else, it might result in more problems like ending up with the wrong partner and the likes.

Work Load

In the olden days, men were characterized to be ones who would go out to work and earn money for the family while the women helped around the home. These days, women work hard and still try to keep the home in place. There is a need to perform well at work, meet deadlines, and still come home to get things coordinated. There may be kids to look out for and other family members. Black women shoulder a lot of responsibilities these days. Having too many responsibilities is destabilizing. The workload can get too much, causing physical and mental stress.

Importance Of Meditation

There has to be a balance between trying to feel beautiful, earning enough money for all expenses, and keeping up with stable health.

Tracking your health and taking good care of yourself will help to guarantee how much you can keep up the hustle in the long run. You do not want to get too engrossed in other things that neglect your health. You would have to do a little bit of eating more healthily, keeping fit, and giving the mind a share of this peace, including meditation. Let's take a look at some of the benefits you can derive from this easy practice.

Stress Management

Meditation serves to release yourself off those thoughts and energy that keep you tensed, stressed, and anxious. When you engage in meditation daily, you feel more at ease. It helps you feel the calm and peace that you would rarely experience with the usual busy endeavors all day long. If you employ this as a practice before bedtime, you would observe that you may have better and well-relaxed nighttime. Meditation in the early hours of the morning can also cause less impact of stress during the day. You will learn to use meditation to channel your mind from the pressures of things that cause you to stress out much. You'll find a better coping mechanism when there is pressure at home, the workplace, or any other gathering.

Perspective To Stressful Situation

You know what they often say about taking a deep breath before letting yourself judge or react to a situation. It is often helpful to help you think twice and see things from a different point of view before you make your judgment. That is what meditation helps you do. It teaches you how to start calm, take a step back and breathe. Breathe out everything that is keeping you furious. This gives you time to think again and analyze things properly. Women who do not engage in such a mindful practice may display more anger issues than the ones that take out time to meditate.

Mindfulness And Self Awareness

Too many times, we become so occupied that er forget to live and enjoy the present. Also, when we begin to face certain issues that we do not seem bold enough to face, we try to distract ourselves. Such distraction might be a quick way to get off the pressure or anxiety we may be feeling. When we begin to practice meditation, we may have to confront whatever we feel at the moment and find ways to get it resolved. Meditation keeps you fully aware of the now, and this will motivate you to make your present a conducive place for you.

Reduction Of Negative Emotions

When we feel stressed or pressured, our minds tend to see the negative aspects of things. This triggers us to become paranoid at every given opportunity. When we try to entertain stress relief exercises like meditation, we allow ourselves to guide our emotions to flow in a positive route rather than the negative. Black women who practice meditation often find themselves becoming realists and optimists rather than pessimists.

Meditation And Illness

Black women find themselves constantly exhausted with work and other physical activities and thoughts from within. The job they need to get done, and their responsibilities to shoulder leave them with little or no time to rest or take care of themselves. They are often worried about things like the monthly books they have to pay for, the outfit they need to wear the next day, and many other problems that need their attention. Their thoughts may even be so detailed enough to worry about the google diagnosis they received about their unusual eye blinking or headache. They often fail to realize that constant worrying about every detail may not be healthy. When the mind is not at peace, we encourage more stress, making us more vulnerable to certain health conditions. You are less aware of what needs to be adjusted in your life as you worry so much about the things that may not matter so much. You may begin to engage in mindless practices that can encourage illnesses. You must always remember that an unstable or unhealthy mind is an unhealthy body. You're a reflection of whatever you have on the inside. When you keep bothering in your head, feeding your mind with thoughts that keep you anxious, you become prone to depression. High blood pressure is associated with too much thinking as well. Meditation exercises can help to keep you far away from such. You'll feel more happy and hopeful when you're relieved of stress and negative thoughts. When you are less stressed about things around you, you become less susceptible to sleeping problems and headaches as a result of tension. Then, you may begin to realize that your mind has intensified most of these situations you have been worrying so much about.

Building Your Meditation Skills

You know you do not have to criticize your meditation skills because this involves continuous practice. The benefits do not just show almost immediately, so you have to take it down and enjoy what you are doing. You may experience a situation where your mind wanders and gets distracted during meditation. It can happen to anyone, whether new to meditation or not. Keep up trying to get your attention back to whatever you were focused on in getting that calmness when this happens. With lots of experiments and time, you'll easily find the style of meditation that works just right for you. There are different steps you may want to analyze thoroughly in practicing meditation.

First, you may want to ask yourself why you need this meditation. This is because several patterns or types of meditation are targeted at benefiting you differently. You may want to know the situation you are in that requires peace and calmness and which pattern of meditation is more suitable. Knowing what you want to achieve from a meditation practice will help you choose the best-suited practice. Based on suggestions from the Mayo Clinic, these are some of the types of meditations enlisted.

- Transcendental Meditation. This form of meditation requires you to put less of any physical effort. You just have to stay quiet and repeat a mantra in a specified way to yourself repeatedly to get that peace and calmness.

- Mantra Meditation. This type of meditation involves you holding on to a word and keep repeating this until you have fully focused. This word has to be repeated until you have fully gotten over the disturbing or distracting thoughts at that moment.

- Visualization. Often called guided meditation, this is targeted at making use of your senses to help get you relaxed. In this type of meditation, you are involved in imagining certain things, places, or situations that may help you relax. It is a memory-guided meditation that makes use of all of your senses.

- Mindful meditation. This type of meditation is focused on you being fully mindful or self-aware of the present. This can help you face all of your current dilemmas and help you digest them rather than distract you from them. You become more focused on your breathing, emotions, and thoughts during this kind of meditation. You just allow them to flow without restraint or any form of judgment.

- Yoga meditation. This requires you to be involved in different kinds of postures and a controlled pattern of breathing. Yoga aims at helping you achieve a more flexible body and mind. You will also learn how to concentrate better.

- Tai chi. This is pronounced as "Tie Chee". It is a pattern of Chinese meditation similar to that of yoga. You must move slowly and elegantly while you pay attention to how you breathe.
- Qi gong. This form merges meditation, physical actions, breathing exercises, and relaxation.

After choosing the type of meditation that is suitable for your situation, it is fine to kick off with realistic goals set. You're still in the process of learning, it wouldn't be ideal just to jump right in and commit to long sessions. You have to progress slowly and allow yourself the time to get used to each stage. You can stick to a 2 minutes daily meditation session and move it up the clock as time goes on. Dedicating yourself and being consistent is not easy, so you mustn't push or rush yourself. Take your time, enjoy those few minutes that you dedicate to it.

You may also want to keep tabs on your progress and get yourself to enjoy the experiences all the way. This will help you feel the impact of the benefits. Follow up the practice and reflect on everything that goes on during that time. There are times when you'll have to face all the bad experiences and emotions that pop up during the sessions. Do not try to push them away, just let them flow. You do not have to pressure yourself as you begin to notice how stressed you have been so far. Just calm yourself, face every emotion, you'll feel better slowly.

If you begin to ask yourself about the things you should focus on at this point, you may want to focus on your breathing as you exhale and slowly inhale.

The Environment For Meditation

Black women often battle the issue of a noisy neighborhood, which hinders you when you're trying to stay focused on something. As well, as the environment can play a key role in practicing meditation, you should know that it can be done anywhere. A beginner may need that serenity and quietness of the environment. A place that gives you that happy energy is fine as a choice. It may be your walk-in closet, an outdoor park, or just your room. So long as it is comfortable for you. You'll notice that as you get so used to this practice, you'll easily be able to get yourself into it in any other place. Like during your morning cleanup routine, on the train, or even at the office. You may find it quite challenging taking out that time to perfect your skills in meditation and recognizing its benefits with your family and kids playing around. If it becomes too difficult or impossible to find a perfect spot, you could opt for a group meditation session.

Yes, there are group meditation centers where those with similar aims get to gather around and observe that quiet time together. Often the mantra type of meditation is employed where everyone would have to direct their focus. The focus may be on a particular sound from gong-like equipment or a word that could be repeated until everyone is fully focused. Such a collective type of meditation has been used in the olden days to usher in dark or ancestral spirits for guidance or some sort of help. For this reason, many people consider this practice a diabolical one rather than a therapeutic one. However, it has become a practice known by many, and its benefit will keep being something to attract more people into accessing it.

Conclusion

Your health cannot be compared to wealth. The former is worth more than you can ever imagine; hence prioritizing it is the best choice you can make for your life. You may seem physically fit but endeavor to prioritize your emotional and mental health. If we constantly continue to neglect the feelings inside and allow in the pressure that comes in daily. Soon enough, we'll begin to reap the impact of the damages this stress and pressure would cause. But, if we try to invest our time and energy into becoming healthy in and out, we would be happy and proud we did so. As a black woman, you look past all of which makes you feel less. You're beautiful, strong, intelligent, and can do everything you set your mind to. Prioritize your sanity, watch your health and make peace with every part of you. You do not need to entertain pressure longer than it should be. Take that time out to give yourself that peaceful mental exercise. Make good use of it and maximize its benefits to the fullest. Be kind to yourself enough to allow things to flow without torturing yourself with your emotions. You'll slowly get yourself into that calm and peaceful state where you'll get a clear head with fewer worries over unnecessary things.

Black People Share Big And Small Ways They're Caring For Themselves

Whether you're seeking for affirmation or inspiration, I hope this list of Black people putting their well-being first provides you with what you're looking for.

1. **Living vicariously through friends who are protesting**

The most painful aspect of the rallies has been not being able to take part in them. I'd definitely be there if I was in Detroit, where I grew up, or New York, where I went to college. That's exactly the sort of person I am. It's been challenging to live vicariously via others when I'm hours away from the nearest demonstration. My method of self-care is to ensure that I am connected to everything through my friends on the front lines who are engaged in demonstrations. I've made an effort to remain in touch with them and make them feel loved and supported.

2. **Unpacking feelings with a Black therapist**

Teletherapy is beneficial to me. I was eventually able to locate a Black therapist that was a good fit for me. I adore her, and I'm experimenting with new methods to remain in touch with friends and family, such as virtual game nights and book clubs. I'm attempting to strike a balance between remaining informed and becoming obsessive. I don't use my phone at night, and I don't open any applications first thing in the morning. Even though I can't address systemic racism on my own, I've been looking for ways to contribute to the cause, such as giving and volunteering, without becoming overwhelmed.

3. Reading hopeful texts by Black authors

While I'm not reading anything from cover to cover right now, I do have Emergent Technique: Shaping Change, Changing Worlds and Pleasure Activism: The Politics of Feeling Good on my bedside table, and I dip into them for inspiration. Both versions are well-loved and annotated, and I keep them on hand for when I need a dose of optimism and soul-care. With all of this going on, my self-care practices—yoga, meditation, relaxation, laughter, words—must fuel, feed, and nurture my soul while also reminding me of the communal goal we're working toward. After a long, difficult week, I turned to page 113 of Emergent Strategy and read: 'We are understanding that we need to become the systems we require—no government, political party, or company will care for us, so we must remember how to care for each other.'

4. Moving her body and journaling

My fiancée, children, and I are spending more time gardening and swimming in our backyard. My alone time consists of maintaining my yoga practice and walking my pets. Journaling has taken a back place, but I still do it on occasion to help clear my thoughts.

5. Staying away from the news and social media

I turn off the news and don't spend as much time on social media as I typically do. I'm worried, irritated, and enraged. I have three Black sons to whom I must speak about the ones who are meant to protect them.

6. Cooking, watching videos, and playing the drums

To take my mind off the news, I've been cooking a lot and experimenting with new foods. That's when I'm alone. I've also been attempting to keep myself entertained by watching Minecraft videos and playing the drums.

7. Talking to close friends on the phone every day

I rely on the help of my pals. I'm staying up later, and when I wake up, I'm filled with rage. To avoid internal strife, I phone my closest pals on a regular basis. We work through our emotions until we are calm enough to go about our business.

8. Photographing the protests

My love is photography. It allows me to communicate with everyone who is revolting without doing anything tough, and it is peaceful. I was apprehensive about taking photographs, but no one has troubled me in the least. It gives me the impression that I am a part of it. I also want people to see what's going on since I've witnessed it all from the front lines. I don't have to rely on what the news tells me. I'm also present.

9. Nourishing his body and connecting with others

Given the challenges of simply existing in the moment, I'm taking self-care more seriously than ever before. For me, this involves maintaining my physical and emotional health, as well as my social relationships. I've started eating more fruit on purpose, and I've drank more smoothies in the last two months than I had in the previous two years. I strive to be more intentional about checking in with friends and family to assure my emotional and mental wellbeing. On the balcony, I also spend daily happy hours with my fiancé and baby daughter.

10. Doing at least one self-care act each day, even as a new mom

COVID-19 could, in fact, teach me new coping abilities. I was nearing the end of my maternity leave, and happily, I was able to return to work from home without having to leave my kid with strangers. I understood how easily I could slide into states of despair and anxiety, and I discovered that the most essential thing to keep me sane was to do things for myself, whether it was going on a walk, picking some wildflowers, cooking my favorite cuisine, or anything. I needed to do something for myself at least once a day. Most lately, doing things for my Black community, such as creating a dialogue, has kept me motivated and alive.

11. Meditating and hugging her children

I turn off social media and the television. Taking a vacation from my computer for a few hours works wonders for me. Then, when it's quiet, I meditate to re-center myself and restore my equilibrium. If that's not enough, I hug and squeeze my twins. This is incredibly soothing for me and quite irritating for them [laughs]. They give me hope. Listening to how they see the world and how they enjoy life gives me a sense of serenity. I know I'm meant to be their rock, but they've been my rock through these trying times!

Take time to check in with yourself, whether you're Black or a non-Black ally, a protester or someone trying to comprehend everything from home. Gardner advises, "Listen to your body and honor what it's telling you." "Does it imply getting more sleep, drinking more water, talking less on the phone, or having fun and playing?" Whatever it is, do more of it while also including other things that will help you. You have the right to look after yourself. You have the right to celebrate peace and pleasure."

WOMEN AFFIRMATIONS FOR CONFIDENCE & EMPOWERMENT

Do you want to feel more in control?

Do you want to boost your self-esteem and confidence? Here is a list of the top daily positive affirmations and inspiring quotations for women looking for personal growth, empowerment, and confidence in order to become their best selves

Affirmations for women to boost their self-esteem:

I am capable of big accomplishments.

I am strong, self-sufficient, and bright.

I take bold steps in the direction of my ambitions.

I'm glowing with self-assurance.

Every day, my self-esteem improves.

I'm getting more and more self-assured.

I have faith in myself and my ability.

I am deserving of big things in my life.

Affirmations that help ladies feel more comfortable:

I'm in love with myself.

I am both attractive and seductive.

People that know me adore and respect me.

I am deserving of joy and prosperity.

I am endowed with exceptional characteristics and abilities.

I'm surrounded by wonderful individuals.

In every aspect, I am supported.

I don't need outside validation.

Affirmations for women to feel more happy and grateful:

I am thankful for the abundance that has come into my life.

I am overjoyed, happy, and in love.

I am grateful to be alive.

Right now, I have everything I need.

I'm getting happy by the day.

I am thankful for all of the blessings in my life.

Affirmations to help women love yourself and body:

I am comfortable in my own flesh.

I'm thankful for my body.

I love the way my body looked.

I have a good attitude toward my image.

I'm growing to love myself more and more every day.

I am content with my body.

I value myself and take good care of myself.

I am a lovely lady.

Affirmations to help women become more successful:

I simply create success and money.

I am confident in my talents.

My choices and actions lead to my achievement.

Attracting greater success comes naturally and readily to me.

I am committed to reaching my objectives.

I'm naturally lured to success and wealth.

Affirmations for black women:

I am a stunning ebony woman.

I am capable of doing everything I set my mind to.

My family loves and respects me.

I am powerful and self-assured.

I'm drawing money and success into my life.

I am a strong and brave black woman.

I am generous and empathetic.

QUOTES & SAYINGS FOR WOMEN

Begin each day with a thankful heart.

Be so joyful that when others see you, they get happy as well.

Set a goal that will motivate you to get out of bed in the morning.

My sweetheart, life is a struggle, but so are you.

Today is a lovely day, and I intend to bring nice things into my life.

It's not only about what you eat when it comes to your health. It also has to do with what you're thinking and saying.

You are more powerful than you realize, and you are gorgeous just the way you are.

What you believe about yourself is far more valuable than what others believe about you.

Life is too short to waste time with those who do not respect, appreciate, or cherish you.

I can't think of a more beautiful person than someone who isn't frightened to be herself.

A positive attitude is contagious, but don't wait for others to catch it. Be a bearer.

Keeping a happy attitude does not guarantee that everything will go well. Rather, it is knowing that you will be fine no matter what happens. First and foremost, love yourself, and everything else will fall into place. To do anything in this world, you must first love yourself.

Happiness is letting go of your expectations of how your life should be and appreciating it for what it is.

The most difficult periods in your life frequently lead to the most memorable moments of your life. Continue your journey. Tough challenges, in the end, make strong individuals.

The greatest "error" you can make in life is to be constantly afraid of making one.

When you are afraid of your challenges, they engulf you. You solve your difficulties when you confront them.

As you start and end the day, be thankful for every little thing in your life. You will come to realize how blessed you really are.

Accept who you are and love who you are. Take care of yourself. Others can sense when you love yourself: they can see confidence, they can see self-esteem, and naturally, people draw toward you.

You must learn to say no without feeling terrible about it. Setting limits is a good thing. You must learn to appreciate and care for oneself. You may suffer numerous setbacks, but you must not succumb to defeat. In reality, it may be vital to experience defeat in order to understand who you are, what you can rise from, and how you can still emerge out of it.

With all that has happened to you, you have the option of feeling sorry for yourself or viewing it as a blessing. Everything is either a chance to grow or an impediment to growth. You get to make the decision.

CONCLUSION

Words have tremendous power, and what we say to ourselves may have a strong influence on our life. I've always been a big believer in affirmations and speaking things into being. So I decided to gather a compilation of uplifting affirmations for Black women written by Black women. I hope you like this compilation and find some solace in the thoughts that have been given.

Do Not Go Yet; One Last Thing To Do

If you liked this book or found it useful, I'd appreciate it if you could leave a quick review on Amazon. Your support is greatly appreciated, and I personally read all of the reviews in order to obtain your feedback and improve the book.

Thanks for your help and support!

Made in United States
Troutdale, OR
02/09/2024

17535365R00117